Snow Job

by

Kelly Fitzpatrick

Snow Job

Cover Art by *RJ Morris*

The Wild Rose Press, Inc.
PO Box 708
Adams Basin, NY 14410-0708
Visit us at www.thewildrosepress.com

Publishing History
First Champagne Rose Edition, 2016
Print ISBN 978-1-5092-1161-6
Digital ISBN 978-1-5092-1162-3

Published in the United States of America

His brilliant blue eyes peeked in
through the partially open window. Snowflakes dusted
his dark lashes. A scarf coiled protectively around his
neck and chin. "Thanks for stopping." He pulled on the
door handle that remained locked.

"Are you dangerous?" she asked him. *An escaped
prisoner would not have straight white teeth, would he?*

"No, ma'am. I'm sure not."

That's what they all say. "But can I trust you?" He
didn't look like a liar. He looked like a gift from that
bitch, formerly known as Mother Nature. The same
Mother Nature who dumped snow on Natalie's
otherwise perfect day. She and the *mother* had tangoed
before. "Can I trust you with my life and my car?"

"Absolutely." Blink. "Without a doubt." Blink,
blink. "Hand to God." He raised his gloved hand to
God, which meant nothing to an Atheist or a Devil
worshipper, she guessed, wondering which category he
might fall into.

She let out a breath. "Will you drive?" Of course,
he'd run his own car off the road. Not a glowing
recommendation to his vehicular proficiency.

"Sure. Happy to." He'd probably agree to just
about anything if it didn't involve walking through a
blizzard. Like walking through hot coals, just for
example. Pledging a particularly vile Fraternity. Black
Friday Christmas shopping at the mall. Not much
sucked more than hiking through a snowstorm.

The locks clicked open, echoing in the cab of her
car like a bullet to the brain.

Kudos for Kelly Fitzpatrick

SNOW JOB was a finalist in the 2011 Maryland Romance Writers Reveal Your Inner Vixen contest, series contemporary category, and the 2011 NW Houston RWA Lonestar writing contest in the series contemporary category.

Dedication

To all those poor souls like myself
who are stressed out by the Christmas holiday,
but still love twinkling lights and peppermint.

Chapter One

The snow floated from the sky like twirling, swirling white ballerinas bent on ruining Natalie Duncan's Christmas.

Snow for effing Christmas! Seriously?

What could be lovelier than a white Christmas? It's what dreams and Hollywood motion pictures are made of. The flakes grew larger, falling faster, putting her windshield wipers to the test. Before long her wipers resembled snowplows, pushing the piles of white aside only to be faced with another deluge of snow.

Natalie punched a button on her radio to free herself from the auditory prison of Bing Crosby crooning the words to *White Christmas*. The next station—static. Better, but not much. In a way, the white noise sounded like a fitting accompaniment to the flakes. She turned the radio down, preferring the sound of her heart drumming wildly in her ears.

Squinting, she could barely make out the blurred red taillights of the car some distance ahead on the winding road through the pass. Nothing visible behind her. So much for getting an early start to outrun the snow the weatherman had predicted for later in the day. *Later. In. The. Day. I'm totally switching networks.*

She lost sight of the car ahead on account of the frozen daggers of dread stabbing the glass in front of her. Occasionally she encountered a car traveling the

1

opposite direction, leaving a spray of white in its wake. She glanced at her cell phone to verify her suspicion of no signal because of the mountainous area or the weather or bad luck. *Who would I call? What could they do?*

She gasped when a semi-truck passed on the left, piercing horn blowing as a warning to her small station wagon. Her gloved grip tightened on the wheel. She hadn't even realized he followed. She failed to grasp how poor the visibility had become in the matter of a few moments.

Assessing her gauges, the car had over a half a tank of gas. Temperature—normal. Oil pressure—fine. Breathing—labored. Heart rate—erratic. She had a spare tire and a roadside emergency kit in the back, along with some Christmas gifts purchased on the shopping trip to Hell. She was a shining example for being prepared for any scenario. Except for the mother of all snowstorms.

The topography in either direction lay blanketed in white, her least favorite color from here on out. In her head she planned a total boycott of the colorless color. Picket fences were destined for green in the future. Walls a rich red tint. She decided to buy only brown eggs from here on out.

Natalie barely made out the tire tracks from the truck that passed moments earlier. Through the windshield was nothing but hypnotic white.

How often do you hear about people freezing to death in their car? Hardly ever. Only because the exhaust fumes kill 'em first. Thoughts of skidding off the road—not being found until spring—crossed her twisted mind. *So many ways to die, so little time.* She passed a cock-eyed sedan left by the side of the road, his hazard lights blinking a cruel warning to others who dared journey on. But what choice did she have? The worst lay behind her. Hopefully.

Before she could add being raped and murdered by a crazed hitchhiker to the repertoire of dark thoughts, she spotted a black dot bobbing along the side of the white road. The dot grew larger as the distance between them closed. Inching nearer, she noted a duffel bag slung over the dot's shoulder and a gloved thumb out soliciting for a ride. He limped, preying on her conscience.

Mind reeling with thoughts of guilt, she crept by him, attention forward. *Do not make eye contact.*

Never in her life had she hitched a ride. Never ever considered picking up a hitchhiker. She also didn't fancy dying alone. *Yeah, it's your lucky day.* She wanted *him* to die with her.

He was just a man experiencing a bad car versus weather day, she told herself, recalling the blinking sedan she'd passed earlier. The weather won. She'd want a Good Samaritan to stop for her under similar circumstances. *And I don't want to be alone.* Natalie did the unthinkable. She flipped on her emergency flashers, careened to the right, and rolled the car to a stop.

The stranded motorist picked up the pace, closing the gap until he was no longer a black dot. He was more of a Navy blue blob in a parka and jeans. She powered down the passenger side window a few inches until the accumulating snow collapsed inward, landing on the seat.

His brilliant blue eyes peeked in through the

partially open window. Snowflakes dusted his dark lashes. A scarf coiled protectively around his neck and chin. "Thanks for stopping." He pulled on the door handle that remained locked.

"Are you dangerous?" she asked him. *An escaped prisoner would not have straight white teeth, would he?*

"No, ma'am. I'm sure not."

That's what they all say. "But can I trust you?" He didn't look like a liar. He looked like a gift from that bitch, formerly known as Mother Nature. The same Mother Nature who dumped snow on Natalie's otherwise perfect day. She and the *mother* had tangoed before. "Can I trust you with my life and my car?"

"Absolutely." Blink. "Without a doubt." Blink, blink. "Hand to God." He raised his gloved hand to God, which meant nothing to an Atheist or a Devil worshipper, she guessed, wondering which category he might fall into.

She let out a breath. "Will you drive?" Of course, he'd run his own car off the road. Not a glowing recommendation to his vehicular proficiency.

"Sure. Happy to." He'd probably agree to just about anything if it didn't involve walking through a blizzard. Like walking through hot coals, just for example. Pledging a particularly vile Fraternity. Black Friday Christmas shopping at the mall. Not much sucked more than hiking through a snowstorm.

The locks clicked open, echoing in the cab of her car like a bullet to the brain.

He stowed his duffle bag in the back while she climbed over the console to the passenger seat, brushing away the clump of snow before settling in to the bucket seat. No way would she step one foot outside the car without a rather large caliber gun to her head, which wasn't out of the realm of possibility. The day was only half over, after all. Funny how her thoughts revolved around guns and bullets and death. A bad sign.

The stranger took a seat behind the wheel and pulled off his gloves with his teeth. Extending his hand, he said, "Russ Crew, at your service."

Accepting his hand, she replied, "Natalie Duncan to *your* rescue." As far as she was concerned, she was the hero—he got to play the part of dude in distress.

He grinned, not at all like a serial killer. More like an underwear model. He might be quite Pillsbury Dough Boyish under his layers of winter garb. His face appeared chiseled-in-marble and gorgeous and a little red from the elements. Not a bad combination.

Russ Crew adjusted his seat to accommodate his long legs and checked the rear and side view mirrors for all the good it would do. Probably just done for show. "You and me against the world." He flashed a reassuring smile before easing the car back onto the road, or what she presumed to be the road. Anything between the trees to the right and trees to the left seemed fair game. "It feels good to be warming up again."

She wrinkled her nose at him. "Heated seats are a gift from God."

"Amen. Halleluiah." He took both hands off the wheel for a split second. His homage to God, she assumed. "I'm a believer."

She gripped her throat in the wake of his reckless antics, but decided not to comment. "I haven't seen another car for ten minutes." Well, besides his stranded vehicle, which would be a bad example, and cruel to mention under the circumstances.

"There's one." Russ pointed at an abandoned compact by the side of the road. Another bad example.

His observation did little to reassure her. "Hands. On. Wheel. Please."

He flashed her a second, equally dazzling smile. "I guess playing the license plate game to pass the time is out of the question. How 'bout I Spy?"

What am I, twelve? "I spy something white," Natalie said flatly. It was a game she'd played many times with her daughter. Playing with him interested her only slightly more than playing the game with Tiffany.

"Is it…is it snow?" he guessed.

"A-maz-ing."

"I should warn you, I'm good at this game." He yanked off his hat, and shook his shaggy head of dark hair. He finger-combed his mane into what resembled a sexy I-just-got-out-of-bed-after-a-night-of-hot-love-making style one might see in a fashion magazine.

Nice fingers. Equally nice mane. *I spy something gorgeous.* "Hands. On. Wheel. Please."

Natalie thought he looked like a bit of a wild, yet handsome mountain man, which struck her as a contradiction. Very rugged with about two-day's growth of stubble on his face. Young, she thought, picturing him enjoying making donuts in the snow with his muscle car after a drunken kegger with his stoner friends. There *was* something quite wise about his features, though. His eyes struck her as intense, or that was wishful thinking. For her purposes all he needed to know was how to drive in adverse weather conditions.

He kept the car at a slow, steady pace. Natalie

sensed he was "one" with the road, not just seeing beneath the snow and hearing it guide him, but feeling the road as well. His eyes darted ahead, behind, and on either side. She almost felt safe in the glow of his Zen driving. Almost.

They passed another car abandoned in a ditch. The safe feeling slipped away like a sweet dream fades when you wake. She muttered under her breath her desire to live to see Christmas. She added New Years to her plea. *Why not?* Valentine's Day seemed like pushing the envelope.

"They didn't have chains or four-wheel drive," he tried to reassure her, bobbing his head toward the deserted car. "We're fine."

Her car veered a few feet before he righted it. Natalie sucked in some air and braced her hand against the dashboard for some reason. Like that would spare her life, when in reality, it would probably snap her wrist bone in a collision.

"Just seeing if you're paying attention. You are." He leaned over and patted her hand that still clung grip-of-death like to the dash, "We're fine. I spy something…something black."

She spotted the bird perched on a telephone pole. "Is it the black crow of death come to mock us?"

He cleared his throat. "You're good at this game, too, I see."

"I spy our deaths in a coffin of twisted steel with flames lapping at our heels at the bottom of the ravine up ahead." She remembered the drop-off from that morning when she'd been headed in the other direction for her misguided Christmas shopping. The steep cliff had worried her then in ideal driving conditions.

"Ravine," he repeated. "Thanks for the heads up."

Bracing herself with one hand against the dashboard again, she grasped the handle above the door with her other hand. She squeezed her eyes shut, a single breath trapped in her lungs. Her body tensed as if she herself were frozen in place. Practice for the real thing.

"You can relax now, Natalie."

She expelled the breath. Her tension refused to ease up any more than the snow did. The flakes stubbornly declined letting up for even one lousy minute. If anything it grew worse. She could be stubborn, too, though. In a test of wills, the storm would lose. This time. Probably. All a person had to do was outlast it.

"I hate snow," she muttered.

"Nobody hates snow. Snow is fun." He glanced at his side mirror. "Usually. You can't have a snowball fight without it. You can't build a snowman without it." He used his fingers to list the many joys of snow. "You can't go sledding without it. You can't make snow angels without it."

"Hands. On. Wheel. Please," she ground out between gritted teeth. Once he did as asked, she sank into the heated seat. "You can't get stuck in a snowdrift and freeze to death without it."

Russ cleared his throat again. "We need music." He pressed the CD button to rid them of the static she'd grown to love. His head bobbed to the sound of the pop music. "Did not see this coming. Had you pegged as more of a classical or jazz fan."

"It's my daughter's CD." Hip-hop-be-bop-rock-rap-and-roll-noise Natalie liked to call it. She also enjoyed singing at the top of her lungs to it, under different circumstances involving solitude and the cloak of darkness.

Her and Russ' eyes locked for a split second. *Eyes. On. Road. Please.* Silently she begged the powers that be to stop him from asking the age of her daughter. She already felt like the equivalent of a dirty old lady being helped across the railroad tracks to Naughtytown by a Boy Scout on a mission to get his gigolo badge. A lean, tall, attractive Boy Scout with two days growth of stubble on his face. Stubble she wanted to rub up against like a bear on tree bark. You know—if she lived.

"Do you have any idea how close to civilization we are, Natalie?" he asked. "I'm not from around here. It'll get dark soon." Assessing the sky, he added, "Very soon."

"Don't you mean how *far from* civilization? At the rate we're traveling, it's pretty far. At least"—she leaned closer and considered her trip odometer she'd set that morning—"at least fifty-five miles or more." Treacherous miles fraught with steep drop-offs, potential black ice, and darkness, she wanted to add but didn't. Natalie decided against being a downer, blowing her chance to say "I told you so" later. With them traveling at a top speed of twenty miles an hour in daylight, drop that to ten miles per hour when the sun went down, it was going to be a long night. How far would her gas hold out under those conditions?

Russ took in a deep breath, letting it out slowly. As she feared, his optimism had been an act to console her, which it didn't. But she appreciated his effort.

"You still think snow is fun?" she asked dryly.

A snowplow lumbered by them headed in the

opposite direction. Didn't take long for the plow to vanish from the rearview mirrors, into the wall of snow.

"A plow," he said. "That's encouraging."

She tugged on his arm. "That sign! Do you see that sign?"

"You mean that thing I can't read because it's covered in snow?"

"Under all that snow is a sign for rental cabins." She saw the advertisement every time she traveled this way, always thinking what a fun little summer vacation spot it would be for her and Tiffany. "Slow down."

Russ slowed to a crawl, while she searched for any hint of a road that might lead them to the cozy cabins in the woods. Visions of crackling fires where marshmallows could be toasted or roasted while sipping brandy-laced coffee filled her mind. He probably saw what she saw, a whole lot of white flanked by trees that stood like sentries, keeping them from shelter.

"If I go down that road," he pointed, "we may not get out. Are you sure about this?"

To thwart his chance at telling her "I told you so" later, she replied, "No. I'm not."

They looked at each other tentatively. Russ Crew smiled. Finding his smile infectious, she returned his smile. They both laughed. She couldn't explain the camaraderie she shared with this total stranger. They were in the trenches together, fighting a common enemy—the elements. A battle she'd fought before and lost.

"Let's do it," he suggested.

Do it? Why not? She shrugged. "What do we have to lose except time and our lives."

"Interesting perspective." He angled the car down

what she guessed was the road that wound a trail through the tall, snowcapped trees.

They bounced along, only occasionally spinning their wheels. Natalie loosened her white-knuckled hold on the handle above her head and breathed deep when the rundown redneck lodge materialized through the snow and trees. To her it looked like an oasis. The cabins in the distance, however, were one small step above camping.

"I don't see any lights on, or chimney smoke." Russ brought the car to a halt outside the log structure. "Let's take a look." He handed Natalie the car keys, which she appreciated and pocketed.

Her car door plowed through the snow when she opened it. They slogged a path through the virgin snow to peek in the window to the darkness inside the lodge office. Maybe the power was out due to the weather. Russ jiggled the door handle. Locked.

"I'll walk around the building, see what's what," he said, limping off.

"You better come back," she demanded, desperately wanting to ask if he was hurting. He could have frostbite, a rock in his boot, or a blister. She had no idea what ailed him. If he expected her to construct a litter of tree branches and drag him out of the wilderness, he had another thing coming. She wasn't that kind of woman. That kind of woman being plucky with plenty of moxie and oodles of optimism under adverse conditions. *Nope. Not me.*

Turning his palms up, he shrugged. "Where would I go?" He had a valid point. The highway was quite a hike.

While she waited, Natalie checked for a door key

in all the usual places. Under a planter, a *Welcome* mat, and above the doorframe. Cold seeped into her clothes through her cuffs and collar. She wrapped her arms around her torso and bounced on the balls of her feet. Wandering onto the expansive, creaking deck, Natalie admired the fading view of a meandering river cutting a path through the valley covered in pristine snow. The vision deserved a place of honor on a Christmas card.

Reaching in her coat pocket, she checked her cell phone. "No signal." She sighed.

Russ emerged from the back of the structure. "Nothing."

"It's beautiful the way the snow is blanketing the ground," she called over her shoulder to him.

"Uh…I suppose."

She snapped a photo for posterity. "I don't think we could have found a prettier place to die if we'd tried." She snapped a photo of him, too. *Why not?*

He snorted a laugh. "That's one way to look at it." Opening the back of her station wagon, he asked, "Do you have a tool kit?"

"A tool kit," she repeated. "I have an emergency roadside kit, complete with jumper cables, flares, a flashlight, and that fix-a-flat stuff." Natalie was the poster girl for emergency preparedness. Not that she knew how to use all of those things. Having them was half the battle. At home she had candles, stockpiles of bottled water, and ready-to-eat food. In place of moxie and pluckiness she had stuff. Disaster stuff.

"Tool kit." He held the kit she didn't know she had up over his head.

Joining him, she asked, "Are you going to save us with a monkey wrench, a twist tie, and some used chewing gum?"

"Do you have a twist tie and used chewing gum?" He glanced sideways at her, pausing for an answer.

"No." She shook her head. "No, I sure don't."

"Then, no, I'm not Macgyver."

You're way cuter than Macgyver. "Then what are you going to do with that hammer in your hand?" It was more of a wimpy tack hammer, but a hammer nonetheless.

"I'm going to break into one of those cabins." He pointed to the string of cabins dotting the bank of the river in the distance. "For shelter."

Whoa, Tarzan. All Natalie heard was "me man, you woman". Who was she to argue? But arguing was sort of in her nature. She assessed every situation and anticipated what could go wrong. So many scenarios tumbled through her head. Her eyes returned to him. She didn't want to spend the night in a cabin with a broken window. Sounded cold.

"Why don't you break into the office where they probably have a phone, supplies and hopefully the keys to the cabin?" she suggested.

His eyes narrowed to tiny slits. "First of all, it's 'we'. We're in this together. And second of all, what are you, some sort of criminal mastermind?"

She shrugged. "I'm cold. When I get cold, I get cranky. When I get cranky, you'll break into Fort Knox to warm me up."

He blinked a couple times before turning his attention to the office door. They both trudged on over to attempt to pick the front door lock. Russ tried a slew of tools. Natalie felt vindicated for her obvious good taste in hitchhikers. She'd picked herself a law abiding one who couldn't break into a tent. Considering the temperature, she sort of wished she'd found a burglar. An escaped convict with flexible morals sounded pretty handy at the moment.

She rubbed her gloved hands together. "How 'bout taking the glass out of the door?" She blew on her hands without results. Seemed the cold could get through the fabric of her gloves, but her warm breath couldn't. "It would go back in easy enough. No harm done."

He stepped aside, eyeing her suspiciously. "Be my guest."

She held out her hand like a surgeon. "Flathead screwdriver."

Russ reached into the toolbox, coming back with the tool she'd requested. He slapped it into her hand.

She pried out the window stops holding the glass in place, making her look handy when nothing could be farther from the truth. The stops were already loose from age and dry rot. It was just a little something she'd picked up from her husband, Duane. For some reason it stuck. If he were still alive, he'd have been super proud of her for thinking of it. Prouder still for flawlessly executing her plan.

They worked in tandem to ease out the glass. Natalie reached through the opening to unlock the door. "Ta-da."

He held out his hand for the screwdriver. "I'm impressed."

Me too. She placed the tool in his hand. "Don't be." She didn't want him to go thinking she was one of those independent women who could take care of themselves. Although she sort of was. Independence had been forced on her and she fought it tooth and nail. She'd rather be like her sister who spent more money at the beauty spa than a senior citizen at the casino slot machines.

Russ turned the knob, shoving the door open. "After you."

No one had to tell her twice. She made a beeline for the phone on the desk. She'd been eyeing it hungrily since they'd gotten there. Not that she'd eat a phone, but pizza delivery wasn't as far from her mind as the pizza parlor probably was from their present location. "No dial tone." She dropped it back in its resting place.

He flipped the light switch with no result. "I think they're closed for the winter."

She found a cabinet holding keys, all numbered for their convenience. She dangled one from her index finger. "We just got lucky, Mr. Crew."

His eyebrows shot up. "If by lucky you mean we're going to rot in prison for breaking and entering, then I'd say you're right, Ms. Duncan."

"I'll leave a note and cash to ease our conscience." Natalie pocketed the keys. No one could begrudge them shelter in a storm.

Russ flipped the breakers in the box with no luck. "I'm pretty sure they're closed for the season. No power, no water, no heat would be my guess. I'd say it's going to be a long night."

Not finding much that would be of any use to stranded motorists, they put the glass back in the door and locked up the office like they'd never been there at all. They trekked toward the cabins, leaving side-by-side tracks in the otherwise undisturbed snow that crunched in an annoying nails-on-chalkboard sort of way.

Natalie pointed. "I like this cabin." They all looked pretty much the same. Shabby. The one she chose was the first they came across. It was closest to the car and the office, its best amenity. She dragged the keys from her pocket and found one labeled with the number one, which matched the wooden number block hanging crooked over the door. She offered him the key to their salvation, knowing with some certainty, Russ being a man and all, he'd want to do the honors.

He sucked in a breath and poked the key in the lock. After wrestling with the doorknob and putting his weight into the task, the door flew open, nearly sending him to the floor. He led the way inside. "I swear it's colder in here than outside." His breath came out in visible puffs in front of him, same as it had outside.

Natalie flipped the light switch for no other reason than for-the-heck-of-it. Opening the icebox netted her nothing. Empty. But it would be tragic to starve to death with a refrigerator full of food, so she had to look. All she found was the stale scent of mildew mixed with cleaning product.

She opened the cupboards one at a time. "No power. No food. Nothing."

"I'm going to start a fire," said her eager Boy Scout wannabe.

"At least there's a little firewood," she muttered. Kindling mostly. It wouldn't last long or heat much, only give them something to do while they waited to freeze to death.

The decor was a shabby mishmash of different era furniture. None from this century. The kitchen hadn't been updated since the late nineteen fifties or early sixties. *Did I think this would be a fun vacation spot?* It was one room only, except for the tiny bathroom she guessed could double as a walk-in freezer.

Not much in the way of privacy. She assumed the couch folded out into some sort of bedbug-infested-mold-scented-squeak-symphony where lumps come to die. So far the cabin smelled only of cold, if cold had a scent, with a slight musty odor that would almost certainly be intensified with heat. She'd suffer the smell in exchange for warmth.

She turned her attention to Russ battling with the inefficient fireplace. "I have some paper in my car," she said. "I'll go get it." From his limp, which grew more pronounced over time, it was the least she could do. "I'll get the first aid kit, too. I think there's some aspirin."

He reached out and grabbed her. He had really long arms, she noticed, her eyes following the path of his arm to his handsome face. Strong fingers looped around her wrist, jolting her libido. Apparently the wrist bone is connected to the pelvic bone. Something they did not teach in school.

"I'll get it," he offered. "I need my duffle bag. There's a blanket in it."

Her internal thermometer rose a couple degrees, picturing them huddled beneath one cover, sharing precious body heat. *I'll bet he has really nice body heat.* Even with her temperature up a couple degrees from lust, she shivered in the frigid room.

Natalie faked a laugh. "Eureka, because there is literally nothing in here resembling a blanket. I saw nothing at the office either. No linens or towels. Nothing."

"I want a refund." He stood, towering over her like a skyscraper. A sexy skyscraper.

Gulp. "I second that." She raised her finger in the air. "We're never coming back to this dump."

"Worst vacation ever," he confirmed, which stung a little. Leaving the highway was her lousy idea. Possibly the worst impulse she'd ever had. And besides, he hadn't given the place a chance.

When he returned with his duffel, a flashlight and her bag of car litter, Natalie already nursed a small flame she'd generated from paper found in her coat pocket, and matches near the end of their life that she'd discovered in the kitchen drawer. He tossed her a granola bar, which she caught in midair.

"Thanks."

"Is there nothing you can't do?" He set his bag by a chair and bobbed his head in her direction.

She wasn't sure if he meant the mid-air granola bar catch, or her wicked fire starting skills. This was not her first fire of necessity. Natural gas and electric heat didn't grow on trees, but firewood did. "Sadly, I can't make dinner out of mothballs, pine cones, and snow," she admitted, ripping into the granola bar offering. "Well, I could but you wouldn't like it. Too bad we don't have a dog."

He snorted at her joke. "Or a small child."

"Yum." They laughed. She liked that he had a twisted sense of humor, same as her. If he were humorless, they'd have to occupy separate cabins and take their meager mothball meals alone. She had used humor to cope with a myriad of not-so-freaking-funny-life-changing-mind-numbing problems in her life. Add being snowbound to the list, which beat the heck out of being on the dangerous roads.

"I also found a Mylar blanket in your first aid kit." Russ tossed the magic emergency blanket that was the size of a panty hose packet onto the couch. "And this quilt."

Her heart sped up, and then nearly stopped as he wrestled a quilt, none too gently, from his duffle bag.

"That's not a quilt," she squeaked.

He assessed the quilt she claimed wasn't a quilt, and then said, "Sure it is. I think I know a quilt when I see one. I wasn't born yesterday."

If she had to guess, she'd say he was born about twenty-five to twenty-seven years ago. Natalie fought to keep her voice level. "It's a work of fabric art." The word heathen nearly came out of her mouth. "It's depression era." And just like her, the bedding was in remarkable shape for its age. A little faded in spots. Only one noticeable repair. She'd negotiated a great price, too. Now his dirty hands were degrading it instead of degrading her.

"But it is a quilt?" he inquired, one eyebrow rising above the other.

"Yes," she whispered, her hands up in a sign of surrender. *Put it down.* "It's too valuable to use though."

Russ gently set the cover on the arm of the couch. "I'll leave it here. In case you get cold tonight."

"I'll never get that cold. And neither will you." Her declaration sounded more like a threat.

He whipped out a bottle of wine from the folds of the quilt, holding the bottle harshly by the neck. "Is this a bottle of wine or a work of art, too?"

"Yes," she hissed. Her sister loved a good bottle of

wine. Or an expensive bottle of wine, at any rate. Didn't matter to Lana if it tasted like it had been sifted through a jock strap, as long as the price was right, the name impressive, and the year brag-worthy.

Russ rolled his eyes and held out his hand. "Keys, please. I think I'll go forage."

She handed over the tangled mess of cabin keys. Once he left again, she pulled off her Uggs, followed by her socks that felt damp but were really mostly cold. She wiggled her toes near the flame and felt herself warming enough to brave removing her hat and scarf.

Panic seized her when the notion of Russ taking off in her car, leaving her behind, popped into her head. She breathed easy when her fingers wrapped around her car keys he'd returned to her earlier. His bag rested nearby. She took a deep breath. They were off the treacherous roads. She had shelter and warmth as long as she didn't venture more than a few feet from the fire. Things could be worse, but not much.

Natalie stretched out on the couch, hugging her arms to her body for warmth, for comfort. The stress of the day had zapped all her energy. The sound of the crackling fire, the smell of wood smoke, and the flicker of the flame soothed her. Trees creaked eerily under the weight of the snow outside, the sound bleeding through the thin cabin walls. Darkness folded into silence into stillness and peace of mind.

And then nothing. Oblivion. That sweet spot between consciousness and sleep.

Next thing she knew, a soft, warm kiss landed on her lips. "Mmmm," she murmured. She snaked her hand into the comfort of shaggy hair, knotting the strands between her fingers. She giggled and cooed.

"Russ." Eyes closed, conscience altered, she could see his sky blue eyes seeking an answer to an unasked question. "Yes," she uttered in a breathy whisper. *Yes, yes, yes.*

His mouth closed in, butting up against hers, teeth nipping and tugging hungrily at her lips. She pulled at his clothes in a frenzy. She could hardly be held accountable for her actions while in a dazed state of semi-consciousness. She dragged her tongue along his bottom lip. *Yum.*

Her back arched off the couch when his hand covered her breast, squeezing lightly. He thumbed the hard nipple poking up from under her sweater and she longed for him to stop playing favorites and give equal time to the opposite peak.

She draped her arms over his shoulders and wrapped her legs around his waist, pulling the hardness in his pants against the heat between her legs. "Ooooh." She giggled as if tipsy, which was very unlike her.

"Natalie," he whispered.

"Mr. Crew." It had been so long since she'd had sex, she was nearly combustible. Still, he'd have to do more than look and talk sexy in order to pop her cork.

He cupped the heated mound between her legs, gently stroking and massaging the ache of desire into a throbbing need. Her heart raced, pumping blood to all her drought-ridden body parts. A sizzle of need burned the length of her spine, heading for the hot spot between her legs.

The door slammed hard. Duane filled the doorway of her dream, hurt reflecting in his eyes.

"Natalie!" Duane yelled.

"I can explain," she said. But she really couldn't.

Chapter Two

Russ pushed through the door his arms loaded with firewood pilfered from a nearby cabin. Not enough to get them through the night. He'd need to make another wood run later. The door slammed shut. He cringed, snapping his attention to Natalie all laid out on the dilapidated sofa. Her eyes flashed open with a gasp and she muttered something about being able to explain. Explain what, he wondered. What followed reminded him of a meow like a kitten, only sexier like a woman. Soft and sleepy and way too alluring, accompanied by a stretch resulting in arching her back off the couch.

"Sorry." He placed a log on the dying coals of the fire and stacked the rest on the floor, careful not to disturb her more than he already had. The drive obviously stressed her.

Her dark hair lay fanned out on the plaid sofa, framing her cheeks, pink from cold or something. Maybe she had a fever. He fought the impulse to brush his fingers along her flushed face. He feared getting scorched by the touch of her skin. Scarred for life by one single encounter. He wanted to smack the romantic idea from his head, blaming his fixation on too much idle time on the road.

Russ watched her chest rise and fall with each deep breath. He'd lucked out hitching a ride with her. Things could have gone differently. He'd bummed a ride with a long haul trucker carrying produce from Idaho, a teenage boy who wanted Russ to repay the lift by buying him a case of beer and last but not least *her*. He'd rather spend the night with her. No contest.

Natalie was beautiful, funny, smart, and had proven herself to be resourceful. She was everything you'd hope to encounter while hitching, but rarely do. He'd met some interesting people on his journey. It had been an adventure for sure. But being stranded with a gorgeous woman while a blizzard raged outside was something he'd only ever read about in Playboy magazine. You know, in the engaging articles.

"Where am I?" Her eyes fluttered.

"Cabin. Woods. Snow," he replied. "Ring a bell?"

"Did you find anything to eat?" she asked lazily, relaxing back into the couch. She smacked her lips together as if parched. The blush slowly faded from her cheeks.

You have no idea. He had an appetite for sweet and spicy Natalie. He mentally slapped himself up side the head. *She's a woman, not a sex object.* Russ pulled a can from his coat pocket. "How do you feel about clam chowder?"

She yawned. "New England or Manhattan?"

He held up the can, reading the label. "New England, and"—he fished a jar from his other pocket, prepared to be her hero—"pickles."

"It beats road kill." Her voice was rough and gravelly and sensual from sleep, making his stomach dip and his jeans tighten.

"That's just what my granny used to always say." He grinned, struggling to be amicable when he really wanted to rub some body parts together with her and start a roaring bonfire.

Natalie didn't return his smile. "Remind me never to accept a dinner invite from your granny."

The gold band on her left hand nearly blinded him with shock and awe. *Why didn't I notice the ring sooner?* Eyeing her gloves drying by the fire answered his question. This was his first sight of her dainty hands, the short nails painted in a pale pink that matched her lips and sweater.

Natalie was married. *Of course she's married.* She mentioned having a daughter. He thought he felt a connection that only transpires between two people open and available to more. He realized now they'd clicked because of the extreme situation they found themselves in. It happens. If there was an attraction, it was one-sided.

Natalie slowly rose from the couch and stretched again. Her chest thrust out as a result. He ground his teeth, trying desperately to rein in his growing attraction. She weaved a path to the kitchen, finding a pan right away. She opened drawer after drawer after drawer. All three of them. "Tell me please it has a pop top, because I'm not finding a can opener."

Russ slid the pickles back into his pocket and pulled the tab on the can. On cue, the top emitted a popping sound, and Natalie sighed contentedly. Her feminine sigh ricocheted around his nervous system. *She's married, moron.*

"Did you check the expiration date?" Holding up her hand, she said, "No. Don't tell me. I don't want to know."

"You'll be happy to know we made it just under the wire." He dumped the soup into the pan she held.

"Best served before February."

"Thank you for that, even if it's a lie." She handed him the pan and pinched the pickles from his pocket like a thief. He'd wanted to muscle the lid open for her, but she managed the feat herself. Plucking a pickle from the jar, she crunched down on it and moaned. "The things we take for granted."

He placed the pan near the glowing coals of the fire. "Such as?" He could guess, but enjoyed the melodic tone of her voice.

"Food, television, being able to go from point A to point B, hot coffee—"

"Cold beer," Russ added.

"A warm bubble bath," she said wantonly. Her gaze seemed held dreamily by the snow falling outside the window.

As far as Russ was concerned, snow fell outside like frozen romance. The weather conjured fantasies of long walks hand-in-hand and cuddling before a roaring fire. Snow was a beautiful sight, reminding him of home and family, holidays and turkey dinner. "Stuffing," he muttered, his hunger getting the best of him.

Coming to her senses, she said, "My daughter must be worried sick." She poked around in her coat pocket, finding her cell phone. Natalie circled the cabin searching for a signal with no apparent luck, based on the frown.

He had no one he cared to call. The memory of the life he left behind was still too fresh. Besides, his phone rested at the bottom of his bag—dead.

He decided not to ask if her husband would be worried. If she were *his* wife, Russ would be worried, although she seemed quite capable. Something her husband probably already knew about her. Russ wanted a few more precious minutes with her before their lives intruded. He wanted to believe they bonded due to more than the perilous situation, even if the attraction was in his mind only.

Natalie groaned and slid the phone into her pocket, giving up on making a call. "Should we eat out of the pan, or shall we be civilized?" she said in a hoity-toity tone he found amusing enough to smile about.

"Let's be civilized. We can even pretend we're at a five-star restaurant in New York City, eating off the finest china." *If only.* What he'd give for a thick steak, potato with everything, and steaming hot bread with butter. Real butter.

She handed him a plastic bowl, a mug, and a bent serving spoon. "Mr. Crew, are you off your meds?"

He stirred at the soup with the spoon. "No, Ms. Duncan, I have a wild imagination." Russ waited for her to correct him with a Mrs. She hadn't before. Would she now, or did she want him to think she was available? Natalie clearly wasn't hiding her wedding band. She wore the precious metal like a badge of honor.

She didn't correct him. Instead, Natalie produced a can of beer from behind her back. "Then make believe this is a very expensive bottle of champagne."

"You've been holding out on me," he accused her lightheartedly, complete with wagging his finger in her direction.

"I planned on waiting until you fell asleep. Then I'd chug it after dark." She wrinkled her nose. "I like you way too much to carry out my evil plan. Sadly, the beer is warm because the freezer is downright balmy compared to the rest of the cabin." She shook her head. "Who puts beer in the freezer, anyhow?"

The same people who'd stay in a dump like this.

When the chowder bubbled, he poured it into the bowl and cup. Russ handed her the bowl with the spoon, keeping the mug for himself. She thanked him and curled up on the couch while he took a place by the fire to sip at his soup. He decided distance was in order. They ate in silence. She offered him the beer. Popping the top, he leaned in and handed it back, allowing her the first drink.

She raised the can to him. "You're taking a huge gamble letting me have the first drink. I never know when to stop."

"I'll risk it."

She took a gulp and closed her eyes. "Best beer ever. The chowder's not bad either."

Curious about his new roomy, Russ asked. "What's your story, Natalie?" Part of him knew her better than he knew himself. He almost gave in to the theory of past lives. That was how connected he felt to her, like she was the missing piece of the puzzle of his life. Probably the way she felt for her husband.

"My story." She sighed before handing him the beer. "Well, my sister collects antique music boxes. Every year our brother Clint buys her one for Christmas." She rolled her eyes. "It's their thing. Anyhow, we scooped a great find on eBay. But...no time to ship, so being a great sister to my brother and an even better sister to my little sister, I generously offered to pick it up." She shrugged at the conclusion of her tale. "The rest is history."

He noted her sarcastic tone, but didn't doubt for a moment she was a great sister, mother, and wife. "Sucker."

"I know, right?" She chuckled. "I should have easily been able to make the trip in a day with time to spare, but..." Natalie made a clucking sound.

"Snow," Russ finished.

He had been fishing for the story of her life, not her Christmas shopping expedition. He wanted to hear about her loveless, crumbling marriage to a man who took her for granted. He wanted to save her, but she struck him as pretty independent, except when it came to driving in the snow. She was a devoted sister, worried mother, an accomplished fire starter, and seemingly experienced at the finer points of B&E. He had no doubt Natalie Duncan was a loving wife too. He tried not to think about what a sensuous lover she might be.

Her body, covered in tight skinny jeans and what looked like a vintage sweater, was curvy in all the right places. The woman had a glow about her. A fire simmered within her and Russ was freezing.

"Your turn, Mr. Crew." She wrinkled her nose at him. "What's your story?"

Russ chuckled. He liked the way she called him teasingly by his surname. He'd been called Mr. Crew plenty in his life, but never with the same flair or subsequent zap of delight to his nervous system as when Natalie said it.

"I...I'm a...a writer." *There. I said it. Out loud.* He finally admitted it to the world. Maybe not the world. She was a start. He'd work up to the world if he and Natalie made it out of this mess alive.

"What do you write?" she asked, unfazed by his admission.

What did he expect? Worship. Fawning. For all she knew, he could write catalog descriptions or assembly instructions for Ikea furniture. Russ sighed, relieved she didn't ask the dreaded "are you published?" question that was sure to make him feel like a failure. "I'm writing a novel."

She licked her spoon. "So are you doing some sort of Jack Kerawack trek across America?"

"I wish. My car broke down a couple states back and I decided it wasn't worth repairing." He felt her curious eyes burning a hole through his psyche. Death stare included. Her face was nothing if not expressive, hiding nothing. "What? What's wrong?"

"Your car broke down about a hundred yards from where I picked you up." Her statement sounded like an order that he should heed—or else.

"You mean the Tercel?" He remembered walking past its frozen, lifeless carcass. Although, taking refuge in the car had crossed his mind. "That wasn't mine."

She sat up, ramrod straight. "I thought I was picking up a stranded motorist."

"You were. You did." Russ tilted his head. "I'd been stranded about four days earlier. That's all."

"You don't understand." Her jaw appeared tight. Her eyes narrowed to slits. "I don't pick up hitchhikers."

"Didn't. Past tense. You *didn't* pick up hitchhikers," Russ corrected her, as if she were one of his students. "Clearly you do because you did. You could always say 'I don't pick up hitchhikers any more. Unless you're planning on picking up hitchhikers in the future, but I don't recommend it. Dangerous. You shouldn't grind your teeth like that either." He should also shut up, he decided. Possibly too late. But really, what could she do to him? Kick him out of the cabin?

"So you just decided to pick up and tramp around the country?" She relaxed back into the sofa, flipping her long dark hair carelessly, glossing over her obvious anger about picking him up alongside the road. "No place to be, no time schedule, zero responsibility? Typical."

"I'm headed to the Pacific Northwest. I should have been there already." His belongings no doubt beat him to his new apartment. "So in all actuality, I'm behind schedule. Also typical. And I've got plenty of responsibility. You have no idea." The weight of potential failure bore down on him constantly.

"The Pacific Northwest, huh." She scoffed, making a face he could only read as aggravation. With him? With herself? "Well, you found it."

Russ needed to soften her annoyance, although he wasn't entirely certain what triggered it, or what would sooth it. "I quit my teaching job, rented a place sight unseen, shipped my things ahead of me and I'm going to write day and night. Seven days a week. 24/7. No distractions." *So there.* He was scared by the life-changing prospect, but decided to fake some confidence.

She raised her eyebrows. "Must be nice."

Tilting his head, Russ asked, "Why are you bustin' my…my…you know, chops?"

Natalie shook her head, dismissing his question and him. "I'm not. No reason. Forget it. It just must be nice to be able to follow your dream. That's all."

"If you must know, it's terrifying," he admitted. "To quit my job, leave my home, my family, my support system." Those were also the very things that kept him from immersing himself in writing. He used them all as crutches. "I was awarded a grant to finish my work."

The news grabbed her attention. "A grant." Her hand stroked the arm of the couch, an action he took as nervousness. "You must be very talented then."

God, I hope so. "I've had some short stories and poetry published, but...but...I'd like to think I've got a little talent." He stood up, taking her empty bowl, carrying it to the sink. He shook off his self-consciousness. Russ turned on the faucet. Nothing. "No water," he reminded himself out loud.

"There's plenty of snow." She rose from her place on the couch and crossed the room to the window. "I can't believe it's still coming down heavy as ever."

He wasn't great at figuring the inner workings of a woman's mind, but guessed the conversation about him being a *typical* irresponsible guy was over. New subject—the weather. He'd embrace the change of topic only because she couldn't hold him personally responsible. *Or could she?*

Russ stuffed his hands in his pockets and joined her at the window. "It's slowed down some."

Somewhere between sharing a meal and sharing their life stories, a wedge dropped from the sky, landing smack between them. She'd been more comfortable with the hitchhiking, Tercel-driving bum, than an up and coming novelist. He thought the news might impress her, put them on somewhat of an even playing field. If anything, the truth infuriated her.

Russ stepped outside to escape her silence. The snow crunched beneath his feet with each step he took. The dark had moved in and completely surrounded them. The only light came from the faint glow of the fire through the cabin window. The moon and stars hid behind a cover of clouds. He scooped a bucket of snow. Returning to the cabin, Russ set the bucket by the heat of the fire and hoped her disposition had changed.

In a few moments they'd have dishwater. *What do I do until then?* "I better go scrounge up some more firewood."

Passing him the flashlight, eyes averted, she said, "Don't get lost."

Yes, ma'am. Basically, she wasn't going to come looking for him if he did. Clearly her annoyance with him lingered. He had no idea how to change her dark mood.

****

Natalie couldn't explain her sudden detachment from Russ.

He was just a man, the same man he'd been in the car. He was the same man she'd rescued from the side of the road, but he wasn't, not really. And truth be told, who rescued who was a source of debate. Suddenly Russ was worldly, adventurous, and well educated. Young with a lifetime of opportunities available. He was talented and she was mediocre at best. Her youth already slipped away while she was busy making ends meet for her and her daughter.

Natalie hadn't finished high school. Her life had been derailed by a life-changing accident involving the captain of the swim team, Duane Duncan. *Duane.* He almost certainly had a part in her aloofness toward

Russ. Her guilt-ridden dream still lingered in her subconscious. Years ago, in a moment of weakness, Natalie and Duane had collided in the backseat of his Buick. They'd named their accident Tiffany.

"Tiff," Natalie mouthed to herself. She touched her ice-cold fingertips to her chapped lips. Tiffany would be worried sick. Yes, she was closing in on adulthood, but to Natalie, her daughter was still a child needing constant care and supervision, maybe more so now than when she was little. Natalie's job was to keep her daughter from making the same mistakes she had.

Russ stomped his feet on the raised wood porch. She extended an olive branch by opening the door in anticipation of his arms filled with wood. *He's got wood.* She snickered to herself and skimmed a few logs off the top of his pile. If nothing else, his eyes conveyed his appreciation. *So handsome.* Nothing could change that. She couldn't alter who he was or who she was. Natalie could only adjust her attitude about how she felt. That was her plan.

He dumped the wood next to the fireplace. "Where's the bucket? I'll get more snow. We might be able to get a couple flushes."

God that sounded practical, like something Duane would have said. Maybe all men thought alike. Thinking of her late husband sent a stabbing pain in the vicinity of her heart, but she shook off the sting.

She touched her hand to her heart. "All my dreams have finally come true."

He cocked one eyebrow over the other. "You'll thank me tomorrow."

"Consider yourself thanked now and we can avoid the awkwardness tomorrow." Natalie was grateful he'd settled right back into a kidding rapport she had to force. "Did you find any more food?" Sure, she was full enough now, but the morning would come soon, making hunger an issue again. At home she had stockpiles of food in the pantry for any emergency. Earthquakes. Windstorms. Flooding rains.

Russ shook his head, failure framing his face. "I'll check the farthest three cabins tomorrow."

"What if there's a fully charged, solar powered espresso-maker, including coffee beans in one of them now?" she asked.

Russ chuckled. "Doubtful." He threw another log on the fire, warming his hands by the flame. "But I do like your optimism."

An optimist wasn't something people customarily called her. Worry wart—yes. Neurotic—sometimes. Duane always said she had a fret fetish. *Duane.* She smiled inside and out. Yes, he was a huge part of her detachment from Russ. The disturbing dream. The hurt in dream Duane's eyes. The guilt in her heart. She shook the nonsense from her mind. She'd done nothing wrong. Yet. Dreaming wasn't a crime. And so what if it was? And so what if she did?

"The mother in me thinks you should get out of those wet clothes." *The cougar buried deep within simply wants you to take your pants off.* She couldn't shake the memory of the naughty part of her dream. And wasn't really sure if she even wanted to shake it, except for the stab of guilt she carried about her subconscious sexual misadventure.

Russ dug through his duffle, dragging a pair of flannel pajama bottoms from the depths. He changed in the bathroom. Upon his return, he shivered from the experience. He burrowed through the bag again, tossing her a pair of long underwear. "Freshly laundered, I assure you."

The thought of sleeping in her clothes was less than appealing, especially knowing she'd have to wear them again tomorrow and possibly the next day. Sleeping in his clothes wasn't even a runner up as far as ideas went. She headed off, if for no other reason than some privacy to think.

"Feel free to use my toothbrush," he called. "Desperate times call for desperate measures."

Natalie skimmed her tongue along her teeth. She barred her teeth to the filmy mirror and decided to take him up on his generous offer. Assessing her reflection, her lips were rough and chapped, cheeks parched and dammit, her gray roots were showing. She'd planned on coloring her hair sometime before Christmas, but something always came up. Tiffany's school choir concert, holiday shopping, housework, not to mention good ol' work work.

Natalie scrubbed her face and brushed her teeth before rinsing her socks and undies in the melted snow that remained. The temperature in the bathroom was not conducive to thinking, as she'd planned, only shivering. Lastly she dumped the dirty water in the toilet and hung her laundry over the curtain rod where no shower curtain dangled.

"Should I send a search and rescue team for you?" he called. At least he didn't ask if she fell in. Duane's favorite saying. She'd always be grateful for Russ' restraint or good breeding.

"Yes, please," she muttered to her reflection. "Come and get me." Natalie rolled her eyes at herself.

"Don't laugh!" she called. Slinging open the bathroom door, she trudged out in his unflattering long underwear that she swam in. This was nothing like her dream. It was no doubt nothing he'd dream about either.

He didn't laugh, but he almost certainly wanted to. *Why does he resemble an underwear model and I look like a back alley bag lady minus the stolen shopping cart?*

They both settled in to watch the flames dance in the fireplace, him from an uncomfortable looking chair, her from the sofa. Natalie sat hugging her knees to her chest. The seriousness of the situation began sinking in. Tomorrow would be Christmas Eve. Natalie had never been away from Tiffany on Christmas. She gnawed on her cuticle. Her sister was probably this very moment filing a missing person's report, threatening the police officer in charge with a lawsuit. And her brother, Clint would be worried about Christmas morning with no music box to present to Lana. Plus he'd be blamed for Natalie's disappearance since she'd been running his errand. *Poor Clint.* Lana could be so unforgiving. About everything.

"What are you thinking?" Russ asked. "You're chewing your lip raw."

"My family." Natalie hugged her thighs tighter to her chest, resting her chin on her knees.

A fist of pressure tightened around her stomach. *I'm trapped.* Not exactly a newsflash. Her reality smacked her right in the gut. Trapped with a hot guy in a confined space. Body heat would be smart and at the same time unwise.

"They're hoping you're safe. You are," he pointed out with a shrug like he'd solved all the world's problems.

If only it were that simple. "Right. I know." She twisted the ring on her finger, stopping only when his eyes locked on her nervous habit. *What would Duane do?* He'd challenge Russ to a belching contest and talk sport's stats. *No! What would Duane do if he'd been trapped in a cabin with a hot super model?* Hopefully her late husband would have talked nonstop about his treasured wife. She snorted a laugh.

"What's so funny?"

She waved her hand. "Nothing."

"What do you do for a living, Natalie?"

Blatant attempt to draw her out of her head, but she guarded herself, physically and emotionally. Not that she thought Russ would make unwanted advances. The opposite was more likely the case. She was a little afraid of making a clumsy pass and being hurt and rejected by him. Talk about awkward.

"Me?" *Yes, you. Who else would he be talking to?* "I own a secondhand store." *Lame.*

She should have made up something more interesting. Doctor. Lawyer. Lion tamer. *Why not?* She'd never see him again after they escaped from Frigid Valley Vacation Rentals. She'd never been any good at lying. With her luck he'd ask her to diagnose a stubborn rash or decipher a tricky legal document. If he pulled a wild lion from his duffle they'd have to deal with bigger problems than lies.

In the absence of an actual fire poker, he poked at the fire with a stick. "How did you get into that business?"

What, am I on a job interview? As his mattress, if there is a God. She snorted again. "I like rummage sales." Natalie shrugged. "Having them and going to them. I found myself in the position of needing to get rid of some stuff." *Like to survive.* He didn't need to know every detail of her past. There was no good way to spin reliance on public assistance and grocery shopping at the food bank. Life had been rough after losing Duane. "It sort of snowballed from there," she said. "No pun intended."

"Natalie." His tone talked down to her, sort of like a small child knee deep in trouble. Russ had caught her red-handed evading his inquiry. He went so far as to lean forward, planting his elbows on his thighs. "I feel a wall has suddenly been erected between us."

He said erected. She swallowed her Beavis and Butthead moment, realizing how much a Beavis and Butthead reference would date her. *I'm so old.* At thirty-five she suddenly felt ancient.

"A wall that wasn't there before," he added.

Because I thought we were going to die. Because I thought you were a regular guy.

"When I met you," he continued, "I felt like I'd known you forever."

"Maybe I babysat you as a child." She smirked to hide a cringe. Natalie couldn't stop herself from pointing out the obvious age difference. As if he hadn't noticed.

He didn't smirk, smile, or show any reaction at all to her flip remark. "Is that what's bothering you?" His brow drew together. "The age thing?"

So he'd noticed, too? Of course he noticed. Squaring her shoulders, she said, "Why should it?" To admit his young age bothered her would be admitting her attraction to him. She'd sooner die. And considering their predicament, dying wasn't off the table just yet.

"I'm older than I look," he said. "More mature than my actual age. Talk to me, Nat."

His choice of nicknames sent a ripple of nostalgia coursing through her body. It was equal parts comfort and discomfort with a side order of guilt. Duane always called her Nat. Not that he'd ever wanted to "talk". Whenever she'd say, "we need to talk", Duane urgently had somewhere else to be with a promise to "talk" later. Avoidance was part of his charm and he'd had lots of charm.

"I...I am talking to you. I have been." She looked away to examine her cracked and brittle nails. "What do you think we've been doing?" *Don't answer that.*

"Avoiding me, my questions, reality..."

I said, don't answer that. "Listen, Russ, I don't remember an adjective from an adverb. I read trashy romance novels that I buy secondhand and love 'em, by the way. In high school we called metaphors metasnores."

"That's funny," Russ admitted without a laugh or a smile, making her doubt his words.

"It's stupid." She waved him off. "It doesn't even make sense."

"No, my high school students would have gotten a kick out of that."

She met his gaze. "High school students?"

"I am...was a high school English teacher." He cringed a little. "I know. Boring. Right? I always wanted to teach. But I knew I had to quit or I'd never finish my novel. And it was just time to move on. You know?"

There was more to that story. She wasn't the only

one erecting walls and creating distance.

"See, you're so smart," Natalie said. He was young, scholarly, and probably gifted. "I'm just a smart ass."

"I'm highly educated, and have the student loans to prove it, but not any smarter than you," he assured her with such conviction she almost believed him. "I admire how quick you think. You are by far the most interesting person I've met in a long time."

Natalie scrunched her face at him, a nasty habit sure to cause premature wrinkles. "Don't get out much?"

"That's beside the point." He chuckled, making her laugh along with him.

Wrinkling her nose, she said, "You're probably very artsy fartsy." She needed more reassurance from him. Why? She didn't know. It wasn't as if they'd fall in love or into bed.

Natalie pictured him sipping wine at gallery openings, visiting museums for fun, and doing crossword puzzles in ink. Okay, yes, she could do that last thing, but her most recent excursion to a museum was Tiffany's fifth grade field trip. Her most treasured art hung from her refrigerator, held up by magnets, signed by Tiffany. Also bemoaned by Tiffany.

Russ inhaled, probably to oxygenate his forthcoming lie. "I have a deep appreciation of art, but I find art in a lot of things like architecture, nature—"

"China and fabric," Natalie said. "The textures. Colors. Patterns." Her hand skimmed the antique quilt resting on the arm of the couch. "Functional art, I like to call it." She loved hand painted china and the craftsmanship of vintage clothes.

He opened his mouth. Maybe to call her crazy or argue. His mouth simply hung open a few seconds. "Sure. Absolutely. China and fabric," he agreed, if not a bit hesitantly. "There's a certain beauty in nature, too—leaves, rocks, even snow."

"Music." She stretched out on the sofa. "Fashion. Cinema. But not movies with subtitles," she was quick to say. "I can't concentrate on the body language and facial expressions when I'm reading the subtitles. See? I'm so dumb."

"Not dumb. At all." He smiled. "I think we have common interests, you and I."

"I love a good western," she blurted, maybe to chase him off or test his hospitality. Natalie half expected he agreed with her for no other reason than she was his ride to civilization once the world thawed out. An excellent reason to stay on her good side. She couldn't trust him to be straight with her, but she could enjoy his lies while they lasted.

"Who doesn't love a western?" His question slid out easily. "How about martial arts flix?"

"I can't get enough of them." Laughing, she added, "But don't tell anyone."

"It's our dirty little secret," he promised. "What's your position on chatting online?"

Natalie scoffed. "Not interested."

"Ditto." Russ relaxed into his chair. "What's with all this text messaging business?"

"I. Have. No. Idea." Natalie laughed. "Don't people just talk face to face any more?"

"Just us." An easy, sexy smile crossed his lips. "I used to spend the first five to seven minutes of every class collecting cell phones from the students."

"Oh, no, tell me you weren't that guy," she said.

He shrugged. "I was."

They talked and laughed until they nearly cried. About many things, long into the night.

"I love Chinese food, but…" Natalie paused, placing her hand on her stomach.

"…it doesn't like me," Russ finished her sentence. "So worth it though."

"Exactly. That doesn't stop me from eating it." She pointed at the dwindling fire. "We need another log." He was closer, plus she sensed he needed to be needed as the fire tender, food finder, and melter of snow. It was a guy thing. Providing and protecting. *Have at it.*

He reached over to place a large knotted log on the coals.

The room became totally drenched in darkness except for the glow from the fire. Natalie watched the light and shadows flicker on his face. Despite the warmth of the flames, she felt the icy grip of guilt for enjoying herself; especially knowing her family must be suffering with worry.

"You're thinking too much again."

She sighed. "I know. That's my thing. I worry." She long ago embraced her fretful nature. Her family never need worry about anything. *Leave the worrying to me.*

He glanced at his watch. "It's eleven-thirty."

"It can't be."

Russ drew closer, displaying his wrist.

"I'm wide awake," Natalie admitted, which flashed like an open invitation to entertain her with his lips or hands. A little of both. Every inch of her felt alive and tingly for the first time in a very long while. He had been so right, whether she cared to admit it or not. She'd experienced a connection to him nearly before she stopped to offer him a ride. The ease that flowed between them, along with a fair amount of chemistry, intoxicated her senses, making her head swim in a fog of attraction. "Tell me about your novel." *Or ravage me. Your choice.*

Russ squinted, his brow crinkling. "Why does that request always make my mind go blank?" He cleared his throat. "It's about love found. And then lost. Because of betrayal. It's one man's search for meaning to his life. Acceptance of his...his shortcomings. No. Wait." He held his hand up. "Acceptance of his failures. Yes, acceptance of his failures. It's about forgiveness of sins. Second chances. Starting over."

"Wow," she mouthed. "That's a tall order. Can I read it?"

"Read it," he repeated, like it was the most absurd idea he'd ever heard.

"I know it's in that duffle bag, Mr. Crew," she drawled playfully.

"It's nothing personal, but I only let strangers read it." He avoided her give-it-to-me-now-or-pay-the-price-later look. He was sly for sure, almost as if he really did know all her tricks.

She scoffed. "Strangers?"

"Agents. Editors." He shrugged.

"I'm practically a stranger." The words slid out of her mouth in a seductive tone she hadn't intended.

He barked out a laugh. "You, Nat, are the polar opposite of a stranger." His admission raised a blush on his cheeks. Probably her as well.

"Maybe someday you'll trust me enough to let me

read it…before it's published, that is." Once published, all bets were off. She'd just buy it and tell everyone she knew him. Being stranded made for a fun party story, if she ever went to parties.

"It has nothing to do with me trusting you," he admitted. "It has everything to do with me trusting myself. It would crush me if you hated it."

She propped her head on her hand. "I promise not to hate it then."

"It would crush me more if you lied to me. So you see," he shrugged, "this is the best way."

"Think about it."

He merely nodded noncommittally.

The last time she checked his watch, it was after one in the morning. Natalie counted sheep on the couch swaddled in her coat and his for warmth and comfort. His woodsy scent comforted and confused her. Russ stretched out on the floor, the Mylar blanket under him. His wool blanket he had in his bag rested over him, and he used his duffle bag as a pillow.

Fear of another guilt inducing erotic dream kept her awake long into the night.

Chapter Three

Russ woke early, cold and achy on the hard floor, a monster of an erection between his legs due to a dirty dream starring Natalie, his naughty snow angel. In his fantasy, Russ licked her dry, which sort of defied logic since his tongue was normally wet. Not this morning. It stuck to the roof of his mouth like he'd been on an alcohol bender instead of drinking only half a beer in the last twenty-four hours.

He stirred the dying embers in the fireplace, placing some kindling on the coals, bringing the flames back to life. The room warmed up, so he hunkered back down and listened to Natalie's steady breath. Sometime during the night she'd broken down and realized the work of art on the arm of the couch was truly a quilt, and used it as such.

He turned his back to her, facing the fire instead. He'd never been tempted to sleep with someone else's wife. He couldn't and wouldn't go there. Russ wanted—no—he needed more than just her body on loan for a short time.

He needed her—all of her—for however long. Having her for a moment in time just wouldn't do, but a relationship born in infidelity wouldn't stand the test of time. He kept hearing the old adage, "If they'll cheat with you, they'll cheat on you". He couldn't go through that again. Common sense didn't stop his desire to kiss her awake, only a change of location would do that.

Quietly he rose, taking his clothes to the bathroom to change in private frigidity.

Her matching bra and panties hung from the shower rod to remind him that *his* clothes covered her naked body like a loose second skin. The realization made him groan. He fingered the pink satin and lace. Cold but dry. If touching her lingerie made him a pervert, he'd just have to live with it.

His first order of business after the panty check involved inspecting the road conditions, which would take more than a single finger. They needed to get out of there before he drove a wedge in her marriage, although he suspected Natalie was too loyal to let him do something so foolish. She'd be the voice of reason and he'd let her take on the role. In his experience, women were far superior in the "reason" department, especially when it came to sex.

Without waking her, he slipped out the door through the slimmest opening possible. The snow creaked eerily beneath his feet with each step. It was the only sound besides the rumble of the river in the distance. And the echo of his conscience banging loudly in his brain like a gong. He scooped up some snow and put it in his mouth. Once it melted, Russ swished the water between his cheeks before spitting it out. His cotton-mouth subsided, but not his desire for the hot mama asleep in the cabin.

In the absence of a cold shower, he'd settle on a long frosty walk.

When Russ returned with an armload of wood, Natalie still snoozed. Her eyelashes fluttered. She sat up slowly and yawned when he noisily placed another log on the fire. Embers rose from the ash only to fade to black. The fire crackled to life. He found the vacant look in Natalie's eyes endearing and knew he was in deep trouble. The kind of trouble that gets you beat up by a jealous husband. He'd never had that happen to him, and wanted to avoid that particular kind of mess for a variety of reasons. Physical pain and bodily injury didn't even top the list.

"It wasn't a dream," she said.

"Being stranded?" He shook his head. "I'm afraid not."

She rubbed her eyes and stretched. "Are we? Still stranded?"

"Completely."

She plopped back against the sofa. "I almost wish someone would come arrest us and cart us off to a warm, dry jail where we'd be entitled to three hots and a cot."

"I walked up to the highway." Russ sat down on the chair, leaning forward with his elbows planted on his thighs. "I was able to flag down a snowplow."

Her fingers covered her lips. "Oh God." She spoke through the spaces between her digits. "Why don't you sound happier about that?" Her hand slowly fell away from her mouth and framed her cheek. "I don't like the look on your face or the tone in your voice."

"The good news is," Russ rubbed his palms together in front of the fire, "the highway has been plowed and sanded. But your car is buried in snow." He cleared his throat. "He's going to send a tow truck."

Her eyes lit up. "That is good news."

"It probably won't happen today."

Natalie let out a loud sigh, making her feelings

known. She wanted out of there, and why wouldn't she? Her family waited. Except for being cold, hungry, and horny, Russ was pretty content. He had time to kill and no one he'd rather kill it with than her.

"That's not all," he said.

She closed her eyes, braced for his next blow.

"The reason the roads were so abandoned was because there was an avalanche behind us. Snow, rock, and mud all covered the highway. The pass was shut down for hours. You were incredibly lucky to get through before it happened." He was surprised they hadn't heard the avalanche. Russ assumed avalanches were loud, but he had no actual knowledge on the matter.

"An avalanche," she muttered, her hands plopping to her lap. "I'm a walking, talking natural disaster magnet."

Russ choked out a laugh. "Why do you say that?"

"No reason." Natalie swallowed hard. "My family thinks I'm buried in an avalanche. My sister will have my memorial planned before we get dug out of here." Staring off toward a dingy wall, she said, "It'll be tasteful and elegant. Lots of flowers. White lilies, knowing Lana. And tears interspersed with anecdotes and spiced punch."

"Sounds nice." He'd rather have a loud wake with plenty of beer and inappropriate stories punctuated with laughter. "I gave the plow guy your name." Russ placed his hand over hers, giving her a little squeeze. Her hands were unexpectedly warm in his. "I don't know if a message will reach them anytime soon. But we can hope."

She covered his hand with her free hand. "I

appreciate the effort, Russ, really I do."

He stole his hand back to place a bucket of snow by the fire to melt. He needed a little space, a buffer between them. She'd feel better after washing the sleep from her eyes. "I'm going to go check the other cabins for that espresso maker you mentioned." He smiled reassuringly at her. If nothing else, he'd like to make her ordeal as comfortable as possible. Maybe he'd find a rusty can of one of those instant breakfasts they could split.

She popped up off the couch, grabbing her clothes from where they rested on a wooden chair. "Wait, I'll go with you." He guessed she had a little case of cabin fever. Who could blame her?

Russ waited, pacing, trying darn hard not to think about her panties, her bra, her naked body in the bathroom surrounded by all that cold porcelain. Either he didn't try hard enough or the task was impossible.

He heard the toilet flush. "Thank you," she called, making him grin and feel a bit like a hero.

He dragged his palm along his whiskers. "You're welcome."

She emerged from the bathroom, covered neck to toe in clothes. Jeans and a turtleneck under what looked like a vintage sweater with pearl-like buttons. The same clothes she'd worn the previous day. All he saw in his imagination was matching bra and panties on her kick-ass figure.

She grabbed her coat. "Let's do this thing."

He opened the door. "After you."

They trudged through the snow, Russ pulling her along behind him. Gloves separated his skin from hers like an unwanted chaperone. His long legs gave him somewhat of an advantage in the deep drifts. The pain in his leg eased a little, causing him to hardly limp at all. The snow was knee deep on her, for him only calf deep.

Each cabin had a small bundle of dry firewood inside and damp wood on the porches. Russ stacked them outside to easily retrieve later. In the next two cabins, besides firewood they collected a can of tuna fish, packets of fast food condiments, a small pillow, and a half a roll of toilet paper. The last cabin was like hitting the jackpot in Las Vegas. Inside was a can of diet soda, two single-serving cans of Spaghetti-Os and a tin of Spam. They opened the medicine cabinet in the bathroom to find dental floss, a sliver of soap, and a single unopened condom. Age unknown.

Russ and Natalie looked at each other. He didn't want to be so bold as to pick up the rubber. He also didn't want to walk back to the outermost cabin in the dark if she felt the urge to huddle against the cold and rub their body parts together to create a little heat and friction. But he would. It could happen. If she thought they might die. The condom looked to him like a divine sign. A holiday miracle.

"Well, merry friggin' Christmas!" Natalie pocketed the dental floss and soap. Lastly she picked up the condom and slapped it in his hand. "Don't say I never gave you anything. I only wish I had a bow to tie around it."

He felt his face heat up. "I'll treasure it."

"Be sure to think of me when you use it." She turned as red as he felt, pivoted and high-tailed it out of the bathroom before he could tell her *that* was a given.

They loaded up on some wood and trekked back

toward their cabin. Without him to tow her along, the depth of the snow pulled Natalie's boots off her feet. It made for a slow return trip. Every time her Uggs came off she laughed. He couldn't help but laugh, too. Giving up, she dropped to the snow in a hysterical fit.

Natalie thrashed around making unruly snow angels in the carpet of white. Sort of like his dream only less erotic and more spastic. She stuck out her tongue, catching falling snowflakes that dissolved on contact. Fearing hypothermia, Russ dropped half his stack of wood and pulled her to her feet, but she fell back laughing. He feared some sort of snow related dementia. Like snow blindness, only it looked more like insanity.

A pile of snow fell from a low hanging branch, landing on his head and sliding down the back of his shirt, making him shriek like a girl and her hoot with laughter. The caterwauling forced a flock of birds to take flight. Russ dropped the rest of his pile of wood to grab a handful of snow, packing it tight between his gloved hands. A snowball hit him square in the chest before he had half a chance.

"Do you really want to start a war?" he asked. "With me?"

His answer was a face full of snow. He retaliated with a hard packed snowball directed at her. Due to her quick reflexes, Natalie rolled, the snow hitting her butt.

"No fair," she squealed. "Help me up."

Assuming a truce, he offered her his hand, hoisting her to her feet. She shoved a handful of snow in his face for his trouble. Natalie ran toward the cabin, leaving her boots behind in a drift. Russ was right on her heels. Her phone beeped just as he playfully caught her about the waist, pulling her to the ground on top of him.

"My phone!" she exclaimed. "I have signal." Scrambling for her forgotten phone, she scrolled through the numbers. She put it to her ear. Giddy, she squirmed on top of him. "It's ringing." She sat up straddling his supine body.

His heart sank a little with the intrusion into their fun. It didn't stop him from enjoying her body on top of his. The mix of warm and cold wasn't altogether unpleasant. Speaking to her family would certainly ease her mind, but he wanted her to himself for just a little longer. Not so much for some hedonistic purpose. He could feed off the memory of their time together for the rest of his life. *The one that got away.* The woman he'd compare other women to, all coming up short.

"It's her voice mail." Natalie leaped to her feet, making for the porch of the cabin where it was drier. "Tiffany, it's Mom. I'm fine. Snowbound, but fine. My cell phone battery is about to die. Don't worry about me. Have a merry Christmas and I love you." Natalie looked at Russ sadly. "Battery is dead. I don't know if she'll get the *I love you* part."

He scrambled off the cold ground, colder now with no Natalie on top for body heat. "I'll bet she knows."

"I should have led with the *I love you,*" she lamented. She shivered, hopping from one foot to the other. "I'm soaked."

"Serves you right." He shrugged. "That's what you get for ambushing me."

She jutted out her lip. God, he wanted to crush his mouth against her pouty lips until she cried for mercy. His desire smoldered inside him, barely contained by generations of civility bred into him. Something primal deep down within him yearned to pin her against a wall with his body and brand her as his property with a playful bite.

"I'll collect the wood and your boots." He shook his head that swam with a flood of desperation and confusion. "You change your clothes before you get sick."

She grabbed the front of his jacket with both hands, pulling him close like she might kiss him. "Then I'll make you the best tuna salad sandwich ever."

"Minus the bread, celery, and onion?" He flashed her his skeptical face and fought the impulse to bury his tongue in her mouth. "Go inside before you catch pneumonia." *And before I devour your bluish lips.*

She let him loose and saluted.

****

Natalie stood in the kitchenette, painstakingly squeezing every drop of mayonnaise out of the condiment packet and into the bowl of tuna fish. She sliced up the last couple pickles, stirring it into the mix.

Her wet clothes dried near the fire. Russ' long underwear covered her bare skin again. While naked, she'd washed with the sliver of soap and used Russ' toothbrush again. After combing her hair, she felt a little more human.

Her heart pounded hearing him on the front porch stacking wood. He stomped his feet at the door in time to her heart thumping in her chest. Her stomach felt like it leaped up into her throat when he pushed through the door. His breath clung in the cold air before dissipating. He immediately crossed the room to place a good-sized log on the dying embers.

The fire sizzled, sparks flying up the chimney. The

sight, sound and smell, all three together warmed her like a placebo.

"Brunch is ready."

"I'm starving," he said, "but let me get out of these wet clothes first."

A shiver of excitement surged through her body at the mere thought of Russ Crew being separated from his clothes. "Don't go into that cold bathroom. Been there, done that." She turned her back to him. "I wouldn't wish it on my worst enemy."

"Please tell me I'm not your worst enemy." The playfulness in his tone tickled her disposition, not to mention her libido.

He made her feel young. Carefree. It had been too long since she'd shared playful banter with a man. Despite the dire circumstances, Natalie was free of responsibility. No store to open and close. No grocery shopping or PTA meetings. Bake sales and bank deposits were pushed to the back of her mind. Getting through to leave a message for Tiffany, even half a message, eased her angst.

"I promise to keep my back turned." She raised her right hand, but also stole a glance over her shoulder. "On my honor."

"On your honor," he muttered. "You forget I've seen how you fight. Hardly what I'd call fair or honorable."

She giggled, more to herself than out loud. She could hear his clothes peeling away. A zipper. The rustle of his jacket. His boots landed on the floor with a thud. She fought valiantly to keep from sneaking a peek at what lay beneath the baggy sweater. Closing her eyes, she imagined a solid chest smattered with dark hair. He probably had a flat stomach with a trail of hair disappearing into his waistband. Her tongue mentally licked a wicked path from his naval to his sternum.

While she waited, Natalie stirred the tuna fish into submission until brunch resembled a smoothie rather than a chunky salad.

"You can turn around now," he said.

Natalie crossed the room with a can of soda in one hand, the bowl of tuna in the other with two forks crisscrossed. She handed the soda to Russ and plopped down on the sofa. She patted the seat next to her. He normally kept his distance by sitting in the chair adjacent the fireplace, but sharing a bowl required proximity.

"I won't bite," she said, a little shocked by the flirtatiousness in her words.

Russ scoffed. "No, you'll probably assault me with a snowball."

If I'm going to assault you, it'll be with my tongue. She tsk tsk tsked him. "Don't be a sore loser, Russ."

He sat cautiously, slowly and as far from her as possible. Maybe he sensed her desire to pounce upon him. "Sore loser," he repeated. "You cheated."

Natalie feigned shock. "Cheated! I never."

"Did you or did you not lay on the ground looking helpless with your cheeks flushed, batting your long lashes at me, your lips pouting like they wanted to be kissed? Then pow! You hit me with a snowball. Hard." His eyes met hers. "That's cheating. Your flushed, batting, pouting image ought to be front and center in the dictionary under the word *cheat*."

"I gotta work with what I have. What I lack in muscle, I make up for in subterfuge." She handed him a fork, mentally deconstructing his words to decipher his meaning. *Is he flirting with me?* Her sister Lana could spot even the most subtle flirtations. Natalie wouldn't recognize flirting if it slapped her in the face. "But I know for a fact I do not bat my lashes. And my lips are nothing if not chapped."

Russ accepted the utensil, dipping it into the tuna. His lips closed around the fork and savored the bite. "This *is* the best tuna fish sandwich I've ever had, bar none. Even without the bread."

Pointing her cutlery at him, she said, "That's the secret to my culinary success. Only cook food for desperate, starving people." Not that any actual cooking took place.

"I insist on making Christmas Eve dinner," he said.

If Russ were anything like Duane, his skills were somewhere between boiled hot dogs and microwave popcorn. Too bad they had neither. "Spaghetti-Os and Spam?" she asked.

"For one reason or another, it'll be a meal you'll not soon forget," he said.

Wrinkling her nose at him, she said, "Because it'll come right back up the way it went down?" She'd noticed a few dents on the cans. That can't be good, she thought.

He pointed his fork at her. "If you're lucky."

"So I'm getting food poisoning for Christmas this year." Her head bobbed. "Good to know."

"You're going to get a spanking this year for Christmas," he said. Russ tossed his fork in the bowl and Natalie's eyes got big in response. "Only you don't have to wait until Christmas morning." He lunged at her to continue the battle they'd fought earlier. He grabbed her waist, tickling her tummy unmercifully.

Natalie squirmed and wiggled beneath his touch, her hands occupied by the bowl, more precious than gold. She used her feet as a protective barrier, shrieking and giggling as his fingers hit their mark.

"Good God, Nat!" He recoiled. "Your feet are like ice cubes."

She slumped into the couch, breathing heavy, her heart pounding. Russ got up and crossed to the fireplace. He tossed a smaller log on the fire and checked the temperature in the bucket of water resting on the hearth.

"My feet are always cold," she said, still gasping for air. "That's nothing new."

He placed the bucket in front of her, plunking her feet in the warm water. "I don't want to hear any complaining out of you."

She relaxed into the couch. "Who's complaining?" It was sort of like a pedicure she'd had once upon a time with Lana.

Russ took his seat, eyes trained on Natalie. She squirmed a little under his scrutiny. If she had to hazard a guess, she would assume her hair was a mess, her face on the verge of a massive breakout, and deodorant was on her Christmas morning wish list. She didn't have an extensive beauty regime, but missed the small comforts of her medicine cabinet back home. Soap. A pink razor. Moisturizer.

"You need someone to take care of *you*," Russ said, quite seriously. "I can tell you're always taking care of other people first; Natalie last, if ever. Am I right?"

She looked away when his words hit the mark. He

wasn't the first person to suggest she get a life. Friends, family, her own daughter recommended she get a life.

"Everyone's needs come before you, from your daughter to your sister to...to your husband," he added.

"Husband?" She automatically twisted the ring on her finger. Natalie wiggled it free, only to slip it snugly back in place.

"Admit it. You're more concerned about them being worried about you than you are about yourself."

She gnawed on her lip, still twisting the damn ring. She knew she was fiddling with it, yet couldn't stop.

He shook his head. "They're all warm and safe and full." Russ lifted one of her feet out of the water. He shook off the water and began rubbing her foot while the other continued soaking. "And here we are cold, our clothes wet. I'd kill for a coffee."

She reclined into the sofa, letting him make sweet love to her foot with his fingers. *He thinks I'm married.* If she told him the truth, would he stop? Would he rub something else instead? Probably not. "My...my husband doesn't worry about me."

He continued punishing her foot to the point of painful pleasure. "That's probably because you're so damn independent."

"I'm so damn independent because he's been dead for six years." She tensed, waiting for his response. Maybe she'd misinterpreted his Boy Scoutishness. She thought he saw her as a little old lady you'd escort across a street. Maybe he saw an unattainable married woman. Natalie feared the inevitable truth. No matter what it was.

His hand squeezed tight around her toes. "You're...you're a widow?"

"That's right," she said. "Don't look at me like I'm breakable. Nothing has changed. I'm the same ol' Nat." She regretted her choice of words.

"Everything has changed," he muttered. "I don't think I've ever met a widow under the age of sixty before."

"We're an elusive, mythical creature depicted in fairytales and movies-of-the-week." She'd always hated the label of widow, but guessed it beat the stigma of *divorcee*. Or maybe not. She assumed divorced women got some action. Everyone treated her like fine bone china when they found out she was widowed. Fragile. Handle with care.

"Can I ask how?"

"How?" She tilted her head and pondered his inquiry. "How what?"

"How he died," Russ said. "Is that too personal?"

Nothing seemed too personal between them. Except that. Talking about Duane, about that day in particular, sometimes brought on tears. Natalie wanted no tears at the moment. "Another time maybe. Okay?"

"Okay." Shaking her revelation from his mind, he asked, "How are your feet?"

Natalie lifted her foot out of the water that now felt tepid at best. "Better." Water dripped from the curves of her arch, plopping into the bucket.

Russ held out his hand. "Give it."

You give it, stud. She wished she had the nerve to say something so brazen. Well, maybe not that, in particular, but something audacious. "My foot?"

Without waiting, he snatched her other foot, giving it a similar treatment to the one resting in his lap. His thumbs pressed into her instep, his fingers curled her toes, working at the joints. "They're still cold."

Other parts of her heated up. She swallowed a dry lump wedged in her throat and realized she'd sort of stopped breathing. She took the opportunity to inhale a deep breath when he rose from the couch, crouching near his bag as he rooted around inside. Coming back to her with a thick pair of wool socks, he took his previous place next to her. Her feet were back on his lap, dangerously close to his crotch. He stuffed her feet into the socks.

Russ returned to the task of quietly rubbing, one foot followed by the other. He broke the silence. "I wish you would have told me yesterday you weren't married."

"Why?" she whispered, the inquiry caught in her throat.

"Because of this." He dropped her feet and wrapped his strong hands around her arms like cuffs, pulling her close. Leaning in, he met her in the middle. His warm lips covered her parted lips, poised for protest. His kiss stopped any objections she may have had. "And this," he murmured against her mouth right before his tongue broke through to twist and twirl with hers.

Russ reclined back into the couch, taking her willingly along with him like a rag doll. Legs and arms and tongues intertwined, trying to inch closer to one another. Her hands slid beneath his shirt, stroking, searching for something. Warmth. Comfort. Safety. What she found was the solid chest she'd fantasized about, along with the mat of soft hair she'd yearned to see and touch. Her fingers combed through the hair, committing the soft feel to memory.

Natalie whimpered into his mouth when his knuckles brushed against her nipples, bringing them to hard peaks.

His hands kneaded and rubbed at her hips, thighs and butt like dough. She expected him to sprinkle some flour on her, toss her in the air and cover her in tomato sauce and cheese. *Someone didn't get enough to eat.* He finessed his thigh between her legs, pulling her center hard against his leg. She moaned, her back arching as she pressed her center along his thigh in a most unladylike fashion.

He doesn't know what he's doing to me, or does he?

Natalie fumbled out of his long-john top, baring her breasts to him. The heat of the moment left her slightly less self-conscious about the perkiness, or rather the lack of perk after breastfeeding. She helped him out of his T-shirt to touch her skin against his. Chest pressing against chest warmed her where their bodies touched, a complete contrast to the cold air on her back and arms, raising bumps. She peppered kisses along his neck, marveling and admiring his torso with her fingers, and then her lips.

He eased his hand past the elastic at her waist of the long underwear and feathered over her skin with his light touch. *Yes, he knows what he's doing to me.* Her legs parted, an open invitation for his fingers, much the same way her lips had parted for his tongue. His index finger wandered lazily through her long neglected folds. Oh, how she wished she'd gotten a bikini wax, but why would she? How could she know she'd be rolling around with a man? A young man.

Her hips rhythmically responded to his finger

stroking the opening to no-man's-land and his palm pressing against her pelvic bone. Her breath hitched like she might choke on her own respirations.

"Before we go any further," she practically panted the words, "can I ask how old you are?"

"Another time," he said. Same as she'd said to him when he asked how her husband died. "Okay?"

Smart man. He probably suspected if she knew the truth—party over.

"Fair enough." She inhaled deeply before launching into another series of heated kisses that swirled around the erogenous part of brain before spiraling down her spine and splashing in her lower belly.

Russ responded to each of her moans with a groan. "I've wanted you...this, since I first laid eyes on you."

"You did?"

The pad of his finger brushed back and forth over the sweet spot between her legs, pulling her closer to total bliss, a place she hadn't been for quite some time. Not with another person in the room, anyhow. "Yes."

She squeaked when his finger eased easily inside her passage. She contracted tight around his digit, holding him prisoner.

"How long has it been?" he murmured. "Since...you know."

"Long, long, long, long time." Her mind was so muddled like in her hormone induced teenage years. "Six years." This was eerily reminiscent of how she'd gotten knocked up way back when. She opened her mouth to yell, "stop", instead saying, "don't stop" when he slipped a second finger inside her.

"So, no pressure on me," he said.

Smiling sweetly down at him, she said, "None whatsoever."

"I'll be gentle," he said.

Natalie moved her hips to his tempo, roiling against his fingers. Her hand snaked past his six-pack abs and into the waistband of his flannel pajama bottoms. *I'm tired of being treated like I ought to be packed in bubble wrap.* "Don't be." She wrapped her fingers around the hardness springing from between his legs.

He groaned and heeded her words, his touch turning urgent. "Is that it?" he asked, breathless, stroking her. "Is that the spot?"

What spot? "Yes." Had to be. Why else would she be so damn hot and losing control of her motor functions? "Oh my God," she whispered. It had been so very long since she'd touched a man, been touched by a man. Too long.

"I want to be inside you," Russ whispered against her neck. He nibbled his way to her ear, lightly biting her lobe. His other hand covered her breast, strumming his thumb at her nipple.

Taking her cue from him, she sank her teeth lightly into his shoulder. She knew that condom was way across the room in his coat pocket. Her lower belly warmed from the spark of an orgasm in the making. "It's too late for that." Her hand squeezed around his shaft and tugged gently. "You just keep doing what you're doing."

He made a hissing sound, drawing air between his clenched teeth. Not only did he keep doing what he was doing, he did it harder, deeper and faster. His tongue shot into her ear. His other hand cradled her bottom, massaging and caressing. He nudged her forward, wrapping his lips around her areola, drawing the nipple into his mouth, swirling his tongue around the tip. The sensation shot directly to her core in a lightning bolt of pleasure.

"Oh yes," she muttered, caught up in the tidal wave of her surging climax. "Russ," she said, choking out his name like a strangled plea. Her thighs trembled and her belly filled with warm, liquid pleasure.

Russ groaned his climax on the heels of her orgasm.

She collapsed limp on top of him, her face buried in his neck. Her free hand combed through his hair. His brow was damp from the exertion of their necking and fondling and groping.

"Baby, baby, baby," he murmured against her temple. His chest heaved against hers, where her heart pounded from exhilaration. "Wow…that was…wow."

"Yeah, I agree." The wave of pleasure he'd gifted defied words or description, but wow worked. "Russ Crew, you are my new best friend." She snickered into his neck, a little embarrassed by her wanton behavior.

"This is way better than text messaging and IMs." He kissed her slowly, sweetly, with less urgency, savoring her lips like a fine wine.

"Without a doubt," she said when the kiss ended.

They lay together for several more minutes. His fingers played in her tangled hair. Natalie lazily stroked his chest and arms. She sank into the space next to him, her butt against the sofa back. They drifted to sleep in each other's arms.

****

When Russ woke, Natalie lay asleep on his arm,

which tingled from lack of blood circulation. *So worth it*. He shivered from the cold, except where his and her bodies met, touched, molded together like two pieces of the same puzzle. He carefully slipped away, intent on sparing her from the frigid temperature by stoking the fire.

"Don't go," she mumbled, her eyes still closed.

Russ kissed each cheek, then her lips. He thought about asking again how her husband died, but clearly it was a raw subject and he didn't want to ruin the mood. "I'll be right back." Besides, she'd ask him again how old he was, which was also a raw subject. To her, anyhow.

When he returned, she sat upright. Her eyes blinked slowly. Natalie rocked the sexiest bed-head hairstyle, as if a professional teased and sprayed it into a ratted mess that fell over her sleepy eyes. She swept the mane off her face. Also sexy.

He pulled her off the couch, into his arms, holding her, swaying.

"Take me dancing," she demanded in a raspy voice, reading his mind.

A slow smile formed on his lips. "Sure, baby."

Cradling her, one arm snaked around her waist, the other curling along her back, he hugged her to him, rocking back and forth in the silent cabin. His mother had made him take ballroom dance as a child. She said he'd thank her one day. He mouthed a silent thanks, although Fred Astaire he wasn't. Russ hadn't seen any use for dance at the time, but the look on Nat's face when he spun her around and dipped her made all the suffering and humiliation worth it. And he would properly thank his mother once he and Natalie were out of this snow-covered mess.

When he lifted her tiny frame off the floor, she wrapped her legs around his waist like a monkey, locking her ankles behind his back and her wrists around his neck. *Yeah, made for each other in every way.*

"I can't believe all the time we wasted when we could have been kissing." To prove his point, he kissed her, pecking and nipping at her plump lips, raw and swollen from kissing.

"And dancing." Natalie laced her fingers at the base of his neck. "Where have you been all my life, Russ Crew?"

"Nebraska."

"Nebraska?" She choked out a laugh. "I figured New York or Chicago. Wherever you came from," pulling herself closer, Natalie planted an affectionate kiss on his lips, "I'm so glad you're here now."

"You and me both." He smacked her bottom playfully, before setting her down. "I have a Christmas gift just for you."

"That's impossible!"

Chapter Four

Russ dug through his bag, pulling out a pile of papers held together with a large binder clip. "It's only the first three chapters, but…but I trust you. I trust me," he quickly added, releasing her from responsibility for his insecurities. He took a deep, cleansing breath to soothe the pounding in his chest and the slight tremor of his hand. "I trust us." Presumptuous perhaps on his part, but he knew she was not someone who would stop over in his life for a short time. Natalie was a keeper and he meant to do just that. Keep her. Whatever it took.

Her hand flew to her heart. "Are you sure?"

Being sure she was a keeper did not equate to being as sure about his writing.

"I most certainly am not." He passed her the pages anyhow, fighting the urge to wrestle them back so she wouldn't find out he was a hack. His biggest fear.

She sank into the sofa. "I know what a huge step this is for you."

You have no idea. Russ didn't share his words with his colleagues, friends, not even his mother. She'd wonder how she failed him if she discovered the dark streak running through her otherwise optimistic son.

Russ and Natalie settled on separate ends of the couch, him pretending to read Hemmingway, because he needed a refresher, her reading his novel. He couldn't concentrate. Her expressive face told no lies, distracting him often. When she chuckled, he could guess where she was in the story. He caught Natalie biting at her lip, even gasping a couple times. But she said nothing, just kept turning page after page.

"I'm going to start dinner," he said. *Why not?* He couldn't focus on his reading. His stomach growled and he could use a double shot of distraction.

Natalie nodded, not looking up from the pages she clutched with both hands. A good sign, he told himself. She read slowly, or perhaps he read fast. Possibly time bent and warped in the wilderness, but not in his favor.

He liberated the Spam from the tin. It made some kind of *plunk* noise, with a hint of *splat* that normally would kill his appetite. Not today. He sliced the loaf of meat with a dull butter knife, laying each slab side-by-side in a heavy, cast iron fry pan.

Pretending to ignore Natalie all curled up on the sofa, like her opinion didn't mean life or death to him, he sat by the fire. He held the pan over the flame.

Turning the last page, she took in a deep breath and let it out slowly. "I...I don't know what to say, Russ."

"You hate it," he guessed. *Why am I such a self-loathing artist type?* Nature of the beast, he decided. Like many artists, he saw himself tortured and persecuted when not narcissistic and self-absorbed. *The world does not revolve around me, my talent, or lack of talent.*

"I don't hate it. It's very intense, very dark, but also quite funny in a twisted sort of way. My favorite way." Her hands caressed the pages, stroking with her fingertips as she spoke. "I love it. Can't wait to read the rest."

He scrutinized her eyes and her body language as

he dissected her words. Russ drew from everything he knew about human nature before saying, "I believe you."

"Who's Valerie?" She tilted her head.

Looking away, he turned his attention to the Spam, flipping it over with a fork. "It's fiction, Nat."

When his stare returned to her, she flashed him a skeptical look. "Clearly it's not. Not entirely. It's too intense...way too real. I have a feeling art is imitating life in a big way within the pages of your writing."

"Maybe I'm a very talented storyteller with a wild imagination." His tone made light of his skills, but he hoped he had a little ability and a lot of luck. He carried the sizzling meat to the kitchenette, putting distance between their banter, hoping detachment would end the painful subject.

"Your talent's not in dispute."

He emptied both single serve sized cans of Spaghetti-Os into a saucepan. Like the Spam, it made an unappetizing *splatish* noise that didn't ease his cravings. "Her name was Vanessa and she *is* the reason I left Nebraska. Or a big part of the reason." He handed the pan to Natalie, avoiding eye contact, not wanting to go into details about how *she* had pretty much chased him from Nebraska with his tail between his legs.

Natalie swung her legs over the side of the couch. Rising, she leaned close, setting the pan near the warmth of the fire. "Can I assume she broke your heart, betrayed you, and cheated on you with your brother?"

He turned and eyed her through a narrowed glare.

"I read the attached synopsis," she said.

"I don't have a brother and she didn't kill my dog either, but the rest is basically true with a little poetic license so no one could mistake her for anything other than the villain." The cheating, betraying, and heartbreaking sort of villain. Putting her crimes on paper was a cathartic exercise not initially meant for publication.

She inhaled deeply. "I must be famished."

He breathed a heavy sigh of relief with a side of sadness that his painful life story was no longer on display. Telling Natalie might have given him closure. He'd thought chronicling his painful past would heal him, but so far—no—not completely. However, the awakening of his long dormant feelings for someone of the opposite sex struck him as a step in the right direction. Russ wasn't sure if it was a case of right time, right place, or was *this* the start of love between him and Natalie? *Is she the catalyst?* His cure for a broken heart? What a heavy cross to bear.

"That smells so good," she added, her eyes closed, which was the best way to enjoy the merits of the meal. Like looking at the sun, best not gaze too long at their dinner. Instead of blindness, Spamghettios brought on a bottomless pit of dry heaves.

"I have many a forte." Russ cut the fried Spam into bite size pieces. Some chunks were quite blackened, while others remained pinkish. "Not just writing."

They divvied up the food, settling together on the sofa, sharing utensils, trading bites, enjoying each other's company more than the actual food. She'd tucked her cold feet under his butt and talked about anything besides the fact that firewood ran low and the food was gone.

"Happy holiday, Nat."

She suppressed a playful grin. "I know this sounds

crazy," she whispered, "but I'm having a great Christmas." He could tell some guilt attached itself to her admission. "Better than the Barbie Dream House Christmas of my childhood."

"Nobody can call it too commercial." He spooned up the last of the food.

She gasped. "I forgot about the bubbly." She shot off the couch, and returned shortly with the bottle of expensive wine, which had no bubbles. Her sister Lana would have to settle for the joy of having her sister back as her Christmas gift. "When I tell Lana we drank her wine, she'll never let me forget it."

She handed over the wine and a corkscrew, one of the few kitchen utensils the cabin did have. The anticlimactic sigh of the cork echoed in the tiny cabin. Due to the age printed on the label, he decided to steal the first drink just in case the wine had turned to vinegar.

He raised the bottle. "To us." He thought about going with Bogart's line, "Here's looking at you, kid", but disdain for plagiarism stopped him, although "to us" had to be stolen from someone. Not knowing who sort of made it easier to steal. Sniffing the wine first, he braved a sip, swishing the liquid around in his mouth before swallowing. "Not bad." He handed her the bottle.

"To the best holiday ever." Natalie sipped her drink.

"To the best Christmas thus far," Russ added. "To many more."

She froze mid-sip, locked in a stare with him and her eyes narrowed.

Yeah, I said it.

She broke off eye contact, and took a long chug. "I don't remember wine tasting so darn good. I'm more of a wine cooler kind of girl."

"You're probably dehydrated." He assessed her for the usual signs. He defied anyone to have anything but dry skin in the weather they'd been exposed to. Fatigue and chills could also be from their environment. Russ reached out to touch her brow. "I should have made sure you're getting enough water." If her heart rate and respirations were elevated or her face flushed, he'd like to think he'd caused that, not lack of fluids.

She made a face. "I don't like the taste of melted snow."

"You mean water?" He cupped her cheek. "Do you feel a fever or headache?"

Natalie brushed his hand away. "I'm fine."

Mood swings. "Drink some more wine," he ordered like a stern taskmaster.

Her eyelashes fluttered. "Are you trying to get me intoxicated and take advantage of me, Mr. Crew?" She took a long gulp of wine and handed it back to him. "I certainly hope so."

"That's merely a happy side effect," he said with a grin he couldn't hide. She seemed fine. All her wits about her. And he was on track to get lucky later, just him, her and his more-than-likely-expired-condom.

"What if I've decided this afternoon was a terrible mistake?" she asked him playfully. Too playfully for him to take her words seriously.

"Get over it. I'm not sleeping on the floor again." His back ached over the previous night.

"How 'bout the chair?" She batted her lashes at him again. "Looks comfy enough."

Russ shook his head. "Then you sleep on it."

"The car?" she said.

As they exchanged lively banter, they passed the wine bottle back and forth, drinking more and faster than they should. "I don't think so, Nat."

"What do you suggest?" Her face was wide-eyed with faux innocence.

He patted the sofa. "I think this couch turns into a bed."

She pointed to the space between them. "This couch?"

He enjoyed her little game. She was going to make him work for it, which was fine. He liked a challenge. She was a jokester and a prankster, some of the things he liked best about her. She was spunky and sassy and he wanted to see more of that side of her. He wanted to see that side of her on the sofa that turned into a bed. Wanted to see it close up. Hear her laughter and taste her silliness along with a little wine.

"You sort of owe me a Christmas gift," he reminded her.

She gasped. "I just this morning gave you a condom."

"Exactly!" Pointing his finger at her, he said, "I'm glad you mentioned that. It's like giving a kid a tricycle with no wheels, or giving a woman an empty jewelry box."

"You gave me half a book." She leaned in to give her words an edge of importance. "Less than half a book."

He got up, took her empty plate and deposited it in the sink. "I gave you so much more than half a book." He gave her his heart and soul. He trusted her and trust did not come easily to him after his last bout with love.

She slumped in defeat. "I know. I owe you. Big time."

Russ flipped the faucet on. Nothing came out. "Why do I keep doing the same thing, expecting a different result?" He hoped history wasn't repeating itself with Natalie. She didn't strike him as a heartbreaker or a cheater, but Vanessa hadn't either. Women all look so innocent until they sucker punch you with treachery.

She shrugged. "Habit."

He crossed the room for the bucket. After dumping the water over the dishes in the sink, he stepped into his boots. "I'm going for more snow and wood."

Natalie turned the bottle upside down, letting the last drops of wine drip onto her tongue. "Bring me back some pumpkin pie, Mr. Crew?"

Grinning, he asked, "With or without whipped topping?"

Her eyes lit up. "Lots of topping, please."

He loved seeing her playful side. Something had changed in her. The weight of the world had lifted off her shoulders. Maybe it was the phone message she'd left her daughter. It might have been the orgasm, or the anticipation of another one shortly, which put him under a bit of pressure to deliver. More than likely the wine set her free.

Russ stepped outside into the biting cold, clutching his jacket around him against the gusting wind whistling through the trees. The brisk air felt good on his face and in his lungs, like a cold slap that forced his senses alive. The moonlight cast a glow on the snowy land around him. He stopped, listening for sounds from the highway, but heard nothing.

He filled the bucket with snow and grabbed an armload of wood. When he entered the cabin, the couch was pulled out into a bed, complete with his blanket draped over the mattress. The sad, lumpy pillow rested in the middle for them to share, unless she banished him to the floor.

Natalie came out of the bathroom. "Is that wood in your arms, or are you just happy to see me?"

He chuckled. "Both."

He laid the damp wood near the hearth to dry. She snatched the bucket, placing it near the fire. They tilted their heads and evaluated the bed in all its lopsided glory. The contraption looked like a deathtrap bent on collapsing beneath their combined weight. *I'll risk it.*

"It already had sheets on it," she whispered. "I choose to believe they're clean."

He nodded, but didn't care one way or the other. Russ had one thing only on his mind. He pulled the condom from his jacket pocket. "I choose to believe this isn't twenty years old." Or degraded from the cold. "I'm afraid to look."

"We have one chance only." She crawled under the blanket, pulling the fabric up to her ears.

"Thanks, Nat. I wasn't feeling nearly enough pressure." As if her admission of zero sex for a long, long, long time wasn't stressful enough. He tossed his coat aside and kicked off his boots. He also hadn't done *this* in a while. Not as long as six years, but before his accident, at any rate. There might be a learning curve, although they managed some spirited necking pretty well earlier in the day.

With her knees pulled to her chest, she said, "Lock

the door, please."

He squinted in her direction. "Who do you think is going to drop by?"

"Escaped inmates from a nearby prison, the police, a tow truck driver, wolves, bears—"

"Okay, okay." He flipped the lock on the front door. The only door. A strong wind would test its wood and rusty metal. He inhaled a deep breath, taking in the beauty of *her* curled up under his blanket. He let the breath out slowly. "I'm going to brush my teeth."

"Keep in mind I'm right here," she called after him. "I'm a sure thing and I'm cold."

"Got it."

Russ took inventory of his reflection in the streaked mirror. *This is no hook-up.* He really respected and admired and valued this woman. A lot. Attraction like this hadn't happened since Vanessa, and that seemed a mere crush by comparison. He recalled how that ended, with his heart through a shredder. Natalie had the means to toss his rehabilitating heart in a blender, torch it with some accelerant, and toss what remained in a nasty dumpster.

Romantic conditions weren't ideal. All the elements worked hard against him. Against them. They were trapped, cold, sometimes wet, forced to eat food abandoned by others. Not exactly the makings of a magical encounter. On the other hand, if Natalie weren't trapped with him, in need of a little body heat, weak from hunger, confused due to dehydration, she probably wouldn't give him the time of day out in the real world.

"Russ!"

"Yeah," he replied over his shoulder through the

closed door. "Be right there."

"I'm going to start without you."

"Don't you dare!" On second thought, he might need all the help he could get. "It's go time," he said to the image staring back at him. Their earlier tryst had been impulsive, bordering on reckless. This, on the other hand, was premeditated sex.

Returning to Natalie, he peeled away his clothes and climbed into the lumpy sofa bed next to her, pleasantly finding her naked. After the previous night on the floor, it felt like a five-star luxury hotel with a king-sized bed. Resting on his side, he snaked his arm under her neck and hovered above her.

She stared up at him. "Just to remind you, I haven't done this—you know—the deed, in a long time. I might be rusty."

He wasn't sure if that meant she wanted to be wowed or she had low expectations, or she didn't want him to have high expectations. "So what you're telling me is that it's been a while?"

Feathering her fingers through his hair, she gazed up at him adoringly. "I love that you listen to me."

"What did you say?" He flinched nearly before she flicked him on the skull with her finger.

"I said—maybe we shouldn't do this." Natalie roughed up his hair. "I said—I'd hate to ruin our friendship."

"Friendship is overrated." It wasn't. The cornerstone of all relationships hinged on friendship, but his wisecrack made her chuckle. Russ quickly rolled to his back, hauling her on top of him as she squealed in delight. Leaning over him, she smiled and his hands framed her face. His lips brushed against hers.

"Wait!" She tugged off her wedding band, and placed it on the side table next to the sofa. He thought maybe she'd decided to call a halt to their play until her lips hungrily returned to his.

Their bodies conformed to one another, separating briefly to shed an article of clothing here and there as they heated up. Legs and arms mingled together. They rolled across the bed in one direction, followed by rolling the other direction, Russ ending up on top, cradled between her legs. He wasn't thinking about tomorrow, just now. They were the only two people in the world as far as he was concerned. The gap in ages disappeared, along with any other differences that divided them.

"Tell me what you want," Russ whispered against her soft lips. A loaded question he might live to regret. The query had backfired on him in the past. He should know better than to ask. But if Natalie wanted a spanking, her feet kissed or anything else within reason, he wouldn't judge, he'd indulge. Happily indulge her. He ground his erection along her crease, pressing and releasing.

She moaned.

"A little of this?" His knuckles traced lazy circles around her bare nipples while he nuzzled her neck.

She drew in a sharp breath. "Yes."

His hand fanned out along her abdomen, snaking down, stopping at the warm juncture between her legs. She parted more for him, welcoming him. "This?" His fingers explored her inside and out.

"Don't stop," she whimpered. "Whatever you do, don't stop."

He had his limits and just about reached them. Desperately he wanted to bury more than his finger inside her. She wanted it too, judging by the way she writhed and moaned beneath him, which only excited him more. He grabbed for the condom and suited up. Russ felt himself losing control even before he eased into her depths, heeding her warning about how long it had been.

He groaned and shuddered, fighting to regain his senses. Russ paused taking a deep breath, but Natalie hooked her legs around his hips and slid against him. She fired hungry kisses at his neck, her hands plowing through his hair and exploring his torso.

She was so sensuous and coated in raw sex appeal. He couldn't believe men weren't hounding her for any scrap of attention. What did she mean by a long time? The woman was obviously starved for physical contact. But surely she hadn't been completely celibate the entire six years. That had to be an exaggeration.

Her hand paused at his hip, tracing the scar that triggered his limp. He half expected her to end their play and drag an explanation from him, but no. She simply gazed into his eyes, the firelight dancing over her pupils. Without missing much more than a beat, she moved against him, fueled by desire that matched his own. He'd almost welcome a respite to regain a little control.

Cupping her hand behind his neck, holding tight, she whispered the word, "Please."

Russ worked his way deeper into her passage and, hopefully, her heart. He busted out all his best moves for her, sucking at her neck and breasts. He scooped under her legs with his arms, spreading her apart, cradling her legs to get closer. All the previous women who'd passed through his bed were preparing him for this one woman. He knew it like he knew his own name. The words "I love you" were on his lips, but saying so would be insanity and relationship suicide.

Natalie's body tensed as if she'd absorbed his silent pledge through her skin. Her fingers gripped at his flesh, nails skimming along his shoulders. Her breath blew out in ragged puffs, same as his.

"That's it," he said. "That's the spot."

"Oh. Yes," she mouthed, seemingly unable to speak in complete sentences. "I think so."

I think so? Russ wanted her to know so. Driving faster, he focused on the rapt look on her face by the dim glow of the fire. A trickle of sweat cut a path down his spine. Eyes closed, her head fell to the side and her back arched. Natalie's orgasm tightened around him. She tumbled into blissful oblivion with him right behind her. He groaned through the dizzying finale.

"Oh. My. God." Her head thrashed back and forth, her hair gloriously tousled around her shoulders. "What have you done to me?"

"Ruined you for all other men, I hope." His heavy breath huffed out against her neck. Kisses followed. She'd ruined him for sure.

"Who was that woman?" Natalie asked. "I didn't recognize her. And I'm sorry if she scratched or bruised you."

"I needed it," he admitted. A little pain to keep him focused on her and her desire. His needs were simple. She satisfied him by her mere presence. He wanted to hover around her, drinking in her scent for the rest of his life. He also wanted to step on the brakes to slow this relationship down, but couldn't. Sensibility was out the door, taking his common sense along.

She clung to him, cradling him between her legs, in her arms, against her breasts. He never wanted to leave her warmth and softness. They shared lazy kisses and tender caresses in the aftermath of their lovemaking.

"What are the chances of doing it again?" she asked.

Squinting, he asked, "Tonight?"

"Now, right now," she replied, her chest still heaving.

"Slim to none."

Her bottom lip jutted out at him.

Russ captured her lower lip between his, tugging. When he released her lip, he said, "If that wasn't our only condom, and if I could rest for an hour or so, I'd say the chances would be better."

Natalie snuggled up in his arms, sharing body heat. He still couldn't believe what just happened, couldn't believe she lay next to him in the aftermath of lovemaking. He'd given up all hope when he'd seen that wedding band.

What a difference a day makes.

****

Russ' gentle kisses woke her the next morning. Natalie's body tingled from his light touch on her skin. "Merry Christmas," he whispered in her ear.

"Hold me, Santa," she said. "I'm cold." Sometime during the night they'd slipped on some clothes, but the layers and blankets were no match for the icy air around them. She exhaled a fog of breath.

"The fire went cold." He spooned her. "No more wood."

She rubbed her bottom into his groin. "Not entirely, Mr. Crew."

"Firewood." He dropped a kiss on her shoulder.

"Russ, how can we be *out* of wood? We're *in* the woods."

"All the wood in the woods is buried under several inches of wet snow," he said. "We have no food, wood, and worst of all, no condoms. It's time to dig the car out and make for the highway. Civilization. The nearest drug store."

"What about the tow truck?" Paying a professional to free them from their prison of snow appealed to her in a big way.

"It's Christmas Day, Nat." His arms tightened around her. "I don't think we can count on a rescue today."

"We're safe here." *Sort of.*

Life outside the cabin remained unpredictable. Sure she needed to get home, even if she didn't entirely want to separate from Russ just yet. The roads were treacherous. The weather precarious. Their relationship seemed uncertain. Not entirely uncertain. It was destined to end, as far as she was concerned. Society, geography, and most of all—time worked against them. She was afraid to ask how much younger he was than her. Better not to know. She guessed him to be on the good side of thirty, her being way past the bad side of thirty.

Natalie wasn't ready for their tryst to end yet though.

Kissing her neck, he said, "Baby, I was up at about four to put the last of the wood on the fire and I heard a snow plow." Russ planted another kiss near her ear. "I watched from that back window," he slung his thumb in the direction of the window, "and I swear I saw headlights. I think the road is open. We just have to get to it."

"I don't know, Russ." She gnawed on the inside of her lip, considering the possibilities. Duane never considered her opinions, always thinking he knew best. *If I had a dollar for every time I could have said, "I told you so."*

He jostled her around playfully. "Trust me."

Considering first Russ was a man and second he was a young man, she had reservations about his better judgment. "What's your plan B? You do have a plan B, right?"

He chuckled and kissed her again. "Plan B is me hiking up to the highway and flagging down a passing motorist."

She certainly didn't want him walking that distance again with his bad leg, although his limp had become less pronounced than the first day when she'd picked him up alongside the road. Natalie had felt the raised scar beneath her fingers the night before. His injury, which she was afraid to ask about, might make him limp, but it didn't affect his lovemaking. Although she didn't want to subject him to a long, cold walk to the road, she also didn't want to volunteer to go instead.

"I can't be rescued like this," she complained. "I look like I've been stranded by a blizzard and sexed up by a hitchhiker. I'm a mess."

He sank into the sofa bed and groaned. "Women."

"What?"

He shook his head. "Nothing."

She yawned. "What time is it, anyhow?"

He checked his watch. "After eight."

"Christmas is ruined. Tiffany has no stocking. She probably won't open her presents until I get home and she's worried sick." More like Nat's sister wouldn't allow Tiffany to open a single gift until Natalie's body is recovered and brought home for a proper burial. Lana was no doubt making everyone's holiday miserable. Another reason to stay put unless she wanted to be caught up in the inevitable misery. Then there would be the guilt trip afterwards for actually being alive and putting them through the nightmarish holiday. It would forever be referred to as the Christmas Natalie ruined.

Damned if I live and damned if I die.

"There are some wet-wipe packets from KFC in the kitchen drawer." Russ patted her rump. "Wash up, run a comb through your hair, and let's get moving so your daughter can open her Barbie Dream House before New Year's."

Natalie sighed and threw back the blanket. "You're right."

"What?" He hunkered under the blanket she flung away. "Hold the presses. Did you just say I was right? I better mark this day in my planner."

"Shut it, mister."

He pulled her back down on the bed. "You seemed so much more charming last night."

She cuddled into his warmth. "It was dark and you *were* drinking." She joked, but Natalie couldn't help thinking she looked a little better under the flicker of firelight and the mind dulling effects of wine. Even jokes had a sliver of truth to them. Once he got a look at her in the daylight, flanked by younger women for comparison, she wouldn't hold up under the scrutiny.

Kissing her, he said, "Then our first stop should be a convenience store for a six-pack."

She swatted him, but he blocked her playful assault.

They got up and dressed. She washed the dishes with what remained of the water from the bucket, while Russ straightened up. He appeared full of energy and eager to get started. Natalie was a little more apprehensive about leaving the sanctuary they'd created. The little cabin seemed magical. Anything was possible. A young, handsome, educated writer could fall for an older, boring, widowed mother of a teenager. That didn't seem possible beyond this snow-covered valley by the stream. Once they were back to civilization, he'd see how ridiculous it was. And she'd see the back of his head as he left.

She sadly resigned herself to the fact that what they'd shared together was coming to an end. He'd sequester himself away to finish his novel and she'd return to her ordinary life; the life she'd been quite satisfied with until she'd been blindsided by the mother of all storms. *I hate you Mother Nature.*

She and Russ would inevitably and slowly grow apart, unless she severed the relationship quick and dirty. She could think about him often, recalling his electrifying touch on her skin until the memory fades like the faint recollection of her husband's touch. And she'd be alone again.

"What are you thinking about?" he asked. His eyes narrowed in her direction.

"Nothing," she muttered.

"Well," he stood with his hands planted on his waist, "everything looks pretty much how we found it."

Glancing around the room, she said, "That's not saying much."

He winked at her. "Let's do it."

Natalie nodded absently, taking in the room one last time like a snapshot keepsake she'd treasure always. It felt almost like leaving the safety and security of a childhood home to go out into the world with all its unknowns. The way Tiffany would leave home soon. Every thought in her head led down a road to loneliness.

Outside the snow spread out like a blanket of white across the ground. The footprints they'd created the other day were erased by wind and more snow. She could barely make out the trail Russ had cut through the woods on his previous trek to the highway.

He bent down. "Hop on."

"You can't carry me," she protested, mindful of the scar and his limp. She felt sure Vanessa had a hand in his lingering pain and permanent scar.

"Sure I can, petite little thing like you. I won't even know you're there."

Natalie giggled and climbed on his back. He carted her across the snow to her car while she hugged his neck tight, afraid of losing him forever. He set her down near the station wagon and assessed the situation. Russ bent and shoved the snow away from the tailpipe with his gloved hand.

Natalie grasped his arm to stop him. "I do hear cars."

"Told you so." He returned to digging. "Start her up, Nat."

"Okay." She dug through her coat pocket for the keys, taking a seat behind the wheel. The leather was cold against her legs. Her breath caught and hung in the air in front of her. She fumbled the key into the ignition and turned it over. The car grumbled to life, but quickly died.

"Try it again," he shouted.

She caressed the steering wheel before turning the key, hoping a little affection would persuade the vehicle to cooperate. The car started with a little more enthusiasm. Natalie patted the dash. When she was sure it wouldn't fail, she hopped out to help shovel snow away from the tires.

"Try to ease the car forward."

Natalie slid back into the seat and did as he requested, but the automobile sputtered and died again. Hanging her head out the open car window, she noticed his concerned look.

"Start her again," he said with a wave of his hand.

It started right up, but the wheels just spun.

Russ waved at her. "Shut it down."

Getting out of the car, she asked, "What now?"

His attention darted around the area. "I might be able to find some branches for traction, but we're likely to have the same problem for the next several hundred yards. I can't dig out the entire road."

"I'll walk up to the highway and flag someone down," Natalie said, resigned now to getting the hell out of there.

One side of his mouth turned up in a half smile. "I'll walk up to the highway and flag someone down."

"I'm a helpless female. I might get more action than you."

He raised his eyebrows. "That's what I'm afraid of, Nat. Besides, I got *you* to stop, didn't I?"

"Yeah, but what are the chances of another desperate, helpless female motoring by, and on Christmas Day?"

Russ scoffed. "Helpless you're not. Desperate either." He leaned in and stole a kiss. "Not any more, anyhow." When she frowned at him, he said, "Don't worry."

"It makes me worry when you say not to worry." In her extensive experience as a worrier, that was the cue to worry.

He turned his palms to the sky and shrugged. "It's Christmas. Someone will stop for a stranded man on Christmas. Otherwise mankind is doomed." Russ kissed her soundly. It was more than a peck, but no tongue. Maybe he was afraid of their tongues fusing together in frozen ecstasy. "Everything will be fine."

Natalie nodded, but felt the weight of impending doom. Impending doom was heavy. She was a little afraid of being abandoned, too. She knew Russ like she knew herself, but isn't that what all women think about a man right before he crushes her world by cheating, deserting, or dying? Not that Duane had done all of those things. One out of three was bad enough, and she hadn't completely forgiven him for dying. Not yet, anyhow.

She was equally afraid of escaping to the real world outside their prison of snow and changing the dynamic of the relationship. People would judge them. Judge her. *What's a handsome, young, talented guy like Russ Crew doing with a middle-aged junk-store owner like Natalie Duncan?* That's what they'd say. People would stare and talk and judge. If she gave them half a chance.

She watched him hike away, only limping a little. His image grew smaller, finally vanishing around a bend where a stand of trees sprouted from the earth. Who was she fooling? The minute he was unburdened by her, Russ would be gone. Maybe not today. Hopefully not today. But soon.

They had a romping good time together. He'd thrown Natalie into the deep end of life. She'd found it so hard to move on after Duane's death, truly move on. Her heart still beat and she continued to breathe. Sure she'd gone on, defining her life as a mother, sister, single parent, and provider. Some of that would be changing soon and Russ was right. She needed to start taking care of her own needs. She pictured herself dining alone and traveling alone. Alone.

Just when she considered tramping back to the relative comfort of the cabin, Natalie spotted a tow truck with a plow affixed to the front making its way toward her. She burst from the frigid car to greet it.

Russ emerged from the passenger side. "Hail the conquering hero."

From the driver's side of the massive truck jumped a tiny man no taller than her. He was balding and leathery, with piercing gray eyes. He struck her as positively feral. And a sight for sore eyes.

"She *is* worth saving," he said to Russ, as he pulled a stocking cap over his shiny dome.

Russ grinned. "I told you so."

The driver lit up a cigar and evaluated the situation from the front, back, and either side of her car. "I'll just yank 'er out. No problemo."

"Yank?" she repeated with concern, glancing back and forth between the two men.

"Natalie," Russ cleared his throat, "this is Eugene." [SEP]

Eugene winked and made a clucking noise.

"The yanker," she said.

Eugene popped the top off a V-8 he pulled from his coat pocket and handed it to her with another wink. Normally she wouldn't drink something pulled from a greasy coat pocket, but thirst and hunger convinced her to not only drink it, she'd chug it even if he'd pulled it from his trouser pocket

"Thank you." The V-8 slid down her throat and couldn't have tasted better if it had been served on silver tray from a crystal goblet with a stick of celery and a splash of vodka.

"Now, pretty lady, when I say yank, what I really mean is yank gently," Eugene said . "I'm an artist."

"A yanking artist?" she said skeptically. *Whatever.* He'd eased her cravings for the moment. She was fully insured. Natalie waved her hand. "Yank away, Eugene."

He gave her a double thumbs-up as he gnawed on his cigar.

"Good decision," Russ said.

"Do you accept Triple A?" she asked.

"I take all major credit cards, young lady, and you can certainly submit to your Triple A for a reimbursement." Wink. "No problemo."

Russ reached for his wallet.

She placed her hand over his hand. "I've got my Visa card."

"Are you sure?" When she nodded, he said, "Okay, then I'm going to go get my duffle bag. Eugene, don't steal my girl while I'm gone."

"No promises." He winked at Russ and returned to the business of yanking her car from the snow.

He indeed proved to be an artist when it came to yanking cars. Eugene was quite capable, not to mention agile and flexible. In no time at all he had her hauled from the snow. She climbed into the warm cab of his tow truck to complete the paperwork, reflecting on the fact that the tow driver was more her age and demographic than Russ.

Eugene was a charmer, for sure, but she couldn't scrape an ounce of attraction for the man. Russ really had ruined her for all other men.

"Could you give this back to your fella?" Eugene handed over a driver's license.

A flash of heat kissed her skin. Hesitating for a second to take the license, Natalie said, "Sure."

Chapter Five

Russ grabbed his duffle bag. He slung it over his shoulder, and then double checked the cabin to make sure the toilet had been flushed, the fire was out, and the place looked at least as clean as they'd found it. Before he closed the front door, he noticed Natalie's ring resting on the side table where she'd placed it the night before in a moment of guilt, or respect, or for her own peace of mind. He scooped it up and slid the band snuggly on his pinky finger for safekeeping. One last fond glance around the place before he secured the door behind him.

He pulled on his gloves. Once he reached her car, he opened the hatch and tossed his bag inside. "You want me to drive?"

She averted her eyes. "Sure."

"I'm just going to drop these cabin keys in the night slot with some cash," Russ said with a reassuring wink.

"I already did that," she said.

He hated that she wouldn't let him pay for anything. He began to feel a bit like a gigolo. More to the point, she treated him as one. Or like a child. He'd prove to her he fell under neither category. "I'll just drop the keys then." He gave Natalie a peck on the cheek. "You didn't fall for Eugene while I was gone, did you?"

Natalie glanced over her shoulder at Eugene sitting in his warm cab, chomping on his smelly cigar. "A little. He's a character."

Clearly something was up. She wasn't herself. The self he knew like he knew the sun would rise and the snow would thaw. She'd slipped into head-to-toe emotional armor while he was away. He'd seen her like this before. He doubted it would be the last time. Her feelings were transparent—the cause of those feelings—not so much.

Russ and Natalie followed the tow truck back to the main road, using his tire tracks to guide them. They waved to Eugene as he headed in the opposite direction to save the next storm victim.

"I need food, a shower, and a change of clothes," Natalie said, "in that order."

A shared shower was on his mind, too. The pleasant idea of spraying her down with warm water that would force her nipples erect brought a smile to his lips. Soaping her up and rinsing her off would be his new favorite pass time.

"The first fast-food drive-thru I see..." *Open,* "I'll stop. Promise." He reached over to squeeze her hand. Russ expected her to reciprocate in some fashion. A squeeze. A pat. Nothing. He returned his hand to the steering wheel. "I figured you'd want to get home asap."

Natalie ran her fingers through her hair. "I do. But I need coffee."

Sensing a distance between them, he focused his attention on the road. She stared out the passenger window, seemingly lost in her thought. In his mind he'd pictured her being happier about liberation from the cabin. He'd imagined gratitude, exhilaration, and relief. Russ fantasized about a reward of affection. Recalling their first few minutes together on the snowy road, he guessed and hoped the treacherous driving conditions had her on edge now—nothing more.

"I think there's a Burger King a couple miles farther," she mentioned.

He glanced over at her. "I doubt it'll be open on Christmas."

Natalie sighed.

A large green road sign listed the five nearest cities and towns, along with the mileage to get there. "Where are we headed?" It amazed him the things he didn't know about her despite the closeness he felt.

"West."

"Where do you live, Nat?" What did he expect? An engraved invitation to Christmas? He'd be a hard guest to explain, but if she asked him to hang out with her for a day or two, he'd happily forgo writing and oblige her. "What's the plan? I'm headed to Peninsula. What about you?"

She squared her shoulders and turned toward him. "Peninsula?"

"Yeah, I'm teaching an American Literature course at Peninsula Community College winter quarter, which starts after the New Year." *I'm free until then*, he wanted to say. His eyes cut to her in the seat next to him.

She was uncharacteristically quiet due to gnawing on her bottom lip. "I thought you were going to write night and day."

"I am." He sensed the past two days unraveling for some reason. All the headway he'd made in the relationship direction suddenly backslid, and Russ had no idea why. "An eight a.m. class will get me up in the morning. I'll have plenty of time to write, a little extra cash and I love to teach." *Why am I explaining myself?*

"I live over by the ocean," she whispered.

The car reeked of sadness, panic, and more than a little uncertainty.

"Natalie, don't worry. We'll manage to see each other on long weekends and holidays." He reached over to caress her thigh. "This isn't over, not by a long shot if that's what you're worried about." That's what he was worried about by her posture and silence.

She fidgeted with her hands in her lap. "Russ, let's face facts. I'm…I'm too old for you."

Returning his hand to the wheel, he said, "Don't start that again."

"I have a teenage daughter who needs my full attention. And…and a business that keeps me very busy. I can't just take off for long weekends."

"What's the name of your business?" he asked, hoping to throw her off a little with the inquiry. If all else fails, change the subject.

"What?"

"The shop, what's the name?" he repeated.

"Oh…uh…The Knick Knack Shack." Taking a deep breath, she resumed listing the reasons they shouldn't see each other. "The shop is open six days a week, so you see I can't just—"

"I'll come to you," he was quick to say. "I have the flexible schedule." Men were known to travel many miles in the pursuit of sex. Certainty that this was more than physical Russ would cross half the state to spend some quality time.

Her head shook back and forth. "I have an impressionable daughter, Russ."

"We'll be discreet." He started to wonder if she wasn't still married. Six years was a long time to still be wearing a wedding ring. "But you shouldn't be living your life for your kid. You need to be happy, too. The happier you are, the happier she'll be."

She nodded, but he sensed she wasn't on board with his parenting advice, especially coming from a guy with no kids.

"Listen, Nat, I know you're feeling stuff…woman stuff that I couldn't possibly understand. I'm trying to though."

"Woman stuff?" She struck an indignant posture. He could tell her mind worked overtime dissecting his every word to throw them back in his face and justify cutting him loose with the label of loser, male chauvinist pig, or the like. Whatever it takes. He'd been on the receiving end of rejection before.

"Mother stuff…widow stuff…woman stuff," he clarified. "We'll exchange phone numbers, let things settle down and we'll talk. Later. Deal?" She needed space. He'd give her a little. Just enough to miss him desperately. Or vice versa.

"Sure, Russ." Her words took on a condescending tone. "Sounds like a plan."

An hour of silent driving followed. Shortly before two o'clock they passed a sign for Peninsula. The roads became clearer and easily passable the closer they got to sea level. He pulled off the highway at a rest stop where hot coffee and cookies were offered to weary Christmas travelers. Since Natalie was familiar with the area, they traded places.

It was half past three when she pulled the car to the curb in front of his apartment. He'd seen nothing but breathtaking scenery for days. Washington was a beautiful state with picturesque landscapes and charming communities. His apartment building was a scab on the otherwise quaint town.

"What a dump." Russ looked up at the bleak structure. It was the perfect place to suffer for his art. "I love it."

"Do you have a key?" she asked.

"They sent it to me Fed Ex." He pulled his bag from her car, slinging it over his shoulder. Russ swept Natalie up in his other arm, giving her the kind of passionate kiss she'd be missing shortly. "I'll call you later." He hoped she'd be more amicable after a long, hot shower, because the coffee hadn't helped her disposition any.

She nodded, touched his face with her icy fingertips and pecked his cheek.

Reluctantly he let her go. Patting his jacket pocket, he said, "I've got your number."

"And I have yours."

"Well, Ms. Duncan, it was a pleasure rescuing you." He winked.

She scoffed. "Excuse me? It was a pleasure rescuing you, Mr. Crew."

"Let's agree to disagree about who did what to whom." His attempt at humor fell between them with a thud. "I'll call you."

She ruffled his hair like he was a child. "Get some sleep."

When Russ reached his apartment on the second floor, boxes lined one wall. He'd planned on arriving before his belongings, but fate and inclement weather had intervened. His first order of business was a hot shower, followed by a hotter meal. First he rummaged around for his cell phone long dead at the bottom of his bag. He plugged the charger into a wall socket and prayed for power. Next was his laptop.

The studio apartment was sparsely furnished with relics of the past, same as the cabin. After the shower, Russ unpacked a few things, and then opened the phone book in search of a restaurant that would deliver on Christmas day. He thought about Natalie still on the road. She'd refused to come in and shower, rest, or eat before continuing.

While he ate Vietnamese cuisine, he listened to phone messages and returned some calls. His mother was worried sick. His father's voice in the background gruffly assured her that Russ was a big boy capable of taking care of himself.

He fought the impulse to call Natalie. He calculated how long until she'd reach the coast. She'd want to spend time with her daughter. She was either enjoying a warm bubble bath, celebrating the holiday with her family or sleeping, which was what he should be doing. Sleep had been a rare commodity the past couple nights.

He knew with some certainty that Natalie's inner voice was telling her that she and Russ were incompatible. He wanted to dispel that voice in her head and reassure her that what happened between them was not a mistake or over.

At eight o'clock that evening he lost the battle and decided to ring her up. Digging through his jacket pocket, he found his driver's license along with her phone number. He got a sick feeling in his stomach, knowing he'd handed the license over to Eugene. His stomach felt sicker when he dialed Natalie only to get a recorded message that the number he'd reached had been disconnected. He verified that he hadn't misdialed.

"She didn't," he mumbled. "She wouldn't."

Russ searched for his laptop, powering it up when he'd found it.

One of the many reasons he chose this apartment was the wireless internet. The other reasons were the location in relation to the college, paid utilities, and the room came furnished, such as it was. The reason he chose Peninsula to begin with was the proximity to Seattle via a quick ferry ride. The many miles separating Peninsula from Nebraska was just a bonus.

Russ searched the internet for Natalie Duncan, Tiffany Duncan, and lastly The Knick Knack Shack. He found nothing helpful. She wouldn't have given him a fake name, would she? Russ had to question everything she'd told him.

He absently twisted the ring around his pinky finger he'd forgotten to return to her. "Shit!"

****

Russ Crew stood in front of the class of college freshmen. He doubted any of them had a burning desire to be there. They all wanted to be doctors, lawyers, or investment bankers. They'd suffer through his community college class to satisfy an English requirement on the cheap before transferring to a university.

His palms sweated a little. First day jitters. He couldn't let them smell his fear. He'd taught plenty of kids. High school kids. These were college kids. He reminded himself they were only a few months older than his former students. He had a couple late bloomers, judging by the faces staring back at him. People working on a second career, or continuing their education to further the career they had.

Teaching college offered him a little more freedom to stray from the course curriculum he'd been tethered to while teaching high school. He could delve deeper into the characters, expect more from his students, and give more of himself. He would inspire them. They could inspire him, test him, challenge him.

He needed to establish boundaries though.

He made the introductions, writing Russ Crew on the dry erase board instead of Mr. Crew. He went over his expectations with his students and explained the class syllabus that had been passed out by a perky red head who was running for the position of teacher's pet.

He already knew the girls would hang on his every word, while the boys struggled to remain awake. Young girls with issues loved his attention. That bothered him when he first started teaching. Now he used it to his advantage to get them to do what he wanted. What he wanted was for them to read and do their assignments. He wanted them to wow him with their passion for literature. Even if they didn't realize their passion for literature until he forced it on them.

"I base my grading on three things." He held up three fingers as he paced before the class. Some kids needed visuals as well as auditory stimulation. If they couldn't remember his words, maybe they'd recall his three fingers in the air. "One. Attendance. Two. Class participation. And three. Homework. There *will* be a final exam, but it's only ten percent of your grade." Russ stopped to face the vacant eyes of his students. "If you come to class and participate, you will not fail. If you are failing, it will not be a surprise to you. I will give you plenty of forewarning and ample opportunity to turn your grade around."

He was unsure if his words were reaching their brains. The boys looked like zombies. By the dazed smiles, the girls appeared to be planning their bridal showers.

"On your syllabus"—Russ held the syllabus up in the air in case they didn't know what it was—"is my email address and my voice mail box number. Do not forward me any chain letters, leave me crank calls, or anything inappropriate." You'd think his request would be common sense, but no. "If you're on the fence about what is and is not appropriate, don't do it. This contact information is for class related questions, comments, and problem. Don't pass it on to your spinster aunt who needs a date to her twenty year high school reunion." That also should go without saying, but his request was based on actual events from the past.

The kids snickered.

"I'm not the school nurse," he continued. "I don't want to hear about a strange rash you've developed."

The kids laughed. Mostly the boys.

"I'm not a trained counselor, so I don't care if you run out of antidepressants. I'm not your friend. I will not lend you money, pick you up from work, or help you move." All lies. He cared too much. Gave too much. "I'm your teacher." He'd been sucked into the *friend* trap, wanting to be the cool teacher. Not again. Hopefully.

Russ introduced them to the book he'd chosen to read. He talked about it briefly, assigned them the first three chapters. Lastly, he took roll call, mostly to put faces to names. It was the first day of class. Some students would run immediately to administration to drop his class, other students would register late and need to play catch up. He dismissed them ten minutes early after twenty minutes of silent reading, but advised them not to get used to an early out.

"Miss Duncan," Russ said. "May I speak to you?"

"Sure." Tiffany Duncan collected her books and approached him as the class filed out of the room. She tilted her head adorably. "Did I do something wrong, Mr. Crew?"

"No, of course not. And you can call me Russ." He propped himself on the edge of his desk, crossing his arms over his chest. He'd nearly tripped over her name during roll call. The asterisks by her name told him she was not a regular student. "So you're my gifted high school student." From what he understood, she'd satisfied her high school credits and was getting a head start on college while waiting to graduate. They'd had a similar program at his high school in Nebraska. The one he'd attended, and the one he'd taught at. He'd also graduated high school early, entering college a year ahead of his peers.

"They don't like to call us gifted," she whispered. "It makes the average kids feel dumb."

Russ chuckled. "Well, we don't want that." She reminded him too much of Natalie. Tiffany even sounded like her. "How old are you?"

"Almost seventeen."

She sure looked like a younger version of Natalie

around the eyes. Her smile was a carbon copy. Looking at Tiffany made him forget how furious he was at her mother. A little.

"How are you fitting in?" College, even community college could be intimidating. "Are you feeling like a little fish in a big pond?"

Hugging her books to her chest, Tiffany shrugged. "I'm only taking a couple classes. So far so good. I don't want to be singled out."

"Got it," he said. "You let me know if you have any problems."

"Like if I develop a rash or need some cash?" She smiled brightly at him.

Russ couldn't help but grin. She was just as flippant as her mother. It never occurred to him that Natalie's daughter would be so…grown up, for lack of a better word. He didn't want to label Natalie as old. He'd pictured a twelve or thirteen year old. No wonder she'd been a little touchy about the age thing. He'd guessed the difference at four to six years, but hadn't wanted to ask. In reality, the difference might be six to eight. Maybe more. Nothing alarming. To him. Clearly he and Natalie did not think alike and it didn't help that she got a look at his driver's license.

"More like if you have any questions or concerns." He suppressed a chuckle. "Anything at all." Russ couldn't help it. She probably thought he was so lame. "Anyone gives you any trouble, tell me."

She wrinkled her nose, same as Nat. "O-okay."

"Your parents must be so proud," he added, hoping for her to slip him some information without him having to come right out and ask direct questions. *Is your father dead? Is your mother available?*

She shrugged again. "I guess."

"I'd love to meet them." *Boy, would I ever.*

Her mouth dropped open. Tiffany's eyes nearly crossed. She looked downright mortified. "I don't think so, Mr. Crew. If she could, my mom would come down here and sit behind me. She's not one hundred percent on board with me taking college classes. She thinks I'm not emotionally equipped." Tiffany rolled her eyes. "As if."

That sounded like the Natalie he knew. "So, are you staying in the dorms or off campus?"

"I wish." Her words dripped with disdain. "I live at home."

His eyebrows shot up. "At home?"

"I'm graduating in June, a year ahead of my class." She shifted her books in her arms. "I'll be lucky if my mom will let me go off to a university before I'm thirty."

Pointing to the floor, he said, "You live here? In Peninsula?"

"Well, yeah. I go to Peninsula High," she said. "I still have to attend there in the afternoon whether I like it or not. I'm a TA, and then I help in the office. Filing and typing. Looks good on the college application, you know." She glanced at the door. "I gotta go, Mr. Crew. I'll be late for calculus class."

"Right." He didn't know what to say. He had a slew of questions that would baffle Tiffany more than he already had. "I'll see you tomorrow, Tiffany. And call me Russ, okay."

She nearly bounced out of the room with youthful exuberance.

He seethed with anger at Natalie's deception after

deception. He wasn't even sure why he was so surprised by this latest lie. He'd spent the last week trying to figure out what he did to chase her away. *Was I too clingy? Did I come on too strong? Am I too young?*

He'd also spent the last week searching for her in the wrong place, when she was right under his nose the entire time. She went out of her way to pointedly deceive to him. And Tiffany didn't mention a dead father when he'd asked about her parents. He tapped the pinky ring against his desk. She was probably missing her ring by now, especially if she really was married.

****

Natalie stirred spaghetti sauce in a pan on the stove. The back door opened and closed, followed by footsteps on the wood floor. "How was your first day of college?" she called cheerily.

She was anything but cheery about her sixteen-year-old daughter being thrown into a sea of eighteen- to eighty-year-olds at the college. Not so much the eighty-year-olds as the eighteen-year-olds.

Stepping into the open and airy kitchen, Tiffany did her one shouldered *whatever* shrug, and said, "Cool."

"Dinner will be ready in twenty minutes."

"Not hungry." Tiffany flipped through the mail on the kitchen counter. "I'm going to a party."

The hell you are. "On a school night, honey? Do you think that's wise?" She'd give Tiffany enough freedom to realize for herself a party on a school night was a bad idea.

"It's a study party," she said.

Does she think I was born yesterday? Smiling

pleasantly, Natalie asked the question she already knew the answer to. "A college study party?"

"Duh, yeah, Mom." She rolled her eyes.

"What happened to asking?"

"Mother, may I please go?" she droned.

Sure, over my dead body. Just throw a sheet over my corpse on your way out. She pursed her lips. "Tiff, honey, sit down." She placed her hands on her daughter's shoulders and gently pushed her to a stool next to the small kitchen island. "I think it's time we had a talk about…you know…about boys and…and sex."

The very subject she'd avoided for many years, both personally and as a parent. What's more, she dreaded it now. Tiffany had always been so studious and emotionally immature for her age. Only within the last couple years had she developed breasts, a menstrual cycle, and more recently, an interest in the opposite sex. *I thought I had time.*

"Sure, Mom." Tiff placed her elbows on the kitchen island in front of her, propping her chin up on her knuckles. "What would you like to know?"

Well, first of all, how do you get over a broken heart? She'd tried ice cream, shopping, and wine, so far. Mostly wine. "I thought you might have some questions for me…your mother…about boys and…or sex." Natalie hoped she had some answers for her daughter. The only thing she knew about sex that she'd like to pass to her daughter was how to avoid it. In the past, the message she conveyed to Tiffany about the subject of sex was *no* and *don't*.

Tiffany looked at her skeptically. "Mom, aren't you about three or four years too late?"

I better not be. "Better late than never."

Rolling her eyes again, Tiffany said, "Your vagina probably has cobwebs."

"Yours better, too," Natalie muttered, returning to her bubbling sauce.

Tiffany gasped. "Speaking of the opposite sex and sex in general, you should see my American literature teacher."

A chill ran a course from the base of Natalie's skull to her tailbone, a visible shudder she hoped Tiffany didn't notice followed. "Oh?" Her "oh" sounded odd in her ears. Unusually high and her voice cracked a bit for one whopping syllable.

"Russ is so funny and totally cool," she continued.

"Since when do you call your teacher by his first name?" Natalie said loudly, to hear her words over the beat of her heart thrumming noisily in her ears.

"He told me to," she protested. "It's college, Mom." There was an unsaid *you wouldn't understand* that Natalie heard loud and clear.

Her daughter's words stung. Natalie had to drop out of high school her senior year to have Tiffany. With a husband and a baby, she'd never gone to college. Changing diapers trumped attending frat parties. She'd packed on some baby weight instead of her freshman ten.

"I'm considering pursuing a major in literature," Tiffany announced.

"I thought you were set on architecture." Natalie didn't want to object too strongly, pushing her daughter into rebellion. Of course, as far as teenage rebellion went, majoring in literature instead of architecture simply to annoy her mother wasn't all bad. It wasn't like turning to drugs, alcohol, or getting knocked up. In the grand scheme of things, she got lucky as far as kids go. "Don't go changing your major just because your teacher is dreamy."

"How did you know he was dreamy?"

I know. Believe me, I know. "You wouldn't be talking about him if he weren't," Natalie said to explain her sudden clairvoyance. "I was sixteen once upon a time." Whether sixteen or going on thirty-six, seemed she had zero sense when it came to men. The best policy was total avoidance.

"A mega-million years ago," Tiff mumbled, "when dinosaurs roamed the earth."

"Tell me about him, this—what was his name—Russ?" She missed him so much. Her heart literally ached from longing. Hearing about him secondhand from Tiffany sent a zing of awareness rocketing through her body. She welcomed the feeling while simultaneously dreading it.

Making a huge sale the other day at the shop, she had this overwhelming desire to share the news with Russ. Same with being cut off in traffic the day before by some guy talking on his blasted cell phone when he should have been paying attention to the road. She'd wanted a little sympathy. From Russ.

"Forget it, Mom." She plucked a grape from a bunch and plopped it in her mouth. "He already warned us about fixing him up with spinster aunts. I can only guess the same goes for widowed mothers."

"Oh, I had that coming," Natalie said, sarcastically. "The way I'm always blatantly chasing after your teachers and all."

Tiffany snorted a laugh. "Sorry. That *was* uncalled

for." Her apology still smacked of insult, whether intended or not. As if the notion of her mother dating was beyond ridiculous.

She'd take the apology. Natalie sort of broke through to the kid below the surface of the teenage cynic who was too cool for school. Too cool for Natalie. They'd once been so close, best friends. Now she was nothing more than a joke to her daughter. It was the natural progression of child distancing herself from her mother in order to fly the coop, leaving an empty nest in her wake.

"When Russ talks, it's with such passion," Tiffany said. "It felt like he was talking just to me. And those eyes. So sharp and intense like he can see my guts right through my skin."

Tell me something I don't know. His ice blue eyes could cut diamonds. His gaze had wrapped itself around Natalie and climbed inside her soul. He was an uninvited squatter in her psyche and she could not evict him. If only she could have convinced Tiffany to drop his blasted class. If she'd pushed any harder, her daughter would have smelled a rat and pushed back just as hard.

"He asked me to stay after class...alone," she added ominously, back to the snotty, teenage Tiffany fighting her mother for independence.

Natalie stiffened her posture. "What?"

Wearing a self-satisfied smirk, Tiffany shrugged at her mother, and then got up and walked away without another word.

Natalie was fairly certain Russ knew full well who Tiffany was when he asked her to stay after class. She didn't have him pegged as a man who chased after young girls. On the contrary, he chased older women. Or maybe she didn't know him at all and he chased all women. And now he had a pretty good idea just how old Natalie was. He was doing a little recon.

Hopefully he'd decided she wasn't worth the trouble and let the matter go. Especially now that he knew how old she really was. She'd made herself quite clear with the fake phone number. She whipped out her cell phone and scrolled to the photo she'd snapped of Russ. The one she'd looked at a hundred times since they parted. She sighed.

Earth to Natalie. "You're not going to any party, young lady," she called.

Chapter Six

Russ drove slowly down Vine Street, taking notice of the station wagon he knew so well parked in the carport. He turned onto Fifth Avenue, parking across the street from the old warehouse. Old it was, for sure, but not shabby except by design. The wooden sign said *Junque Décor*. Beneath that in smaller letters read, *where all things old are new again.*

Charming.

Natalie never failed to amaze him. She was bright and beautiful and amusing and…Russ reminded himself he didn't track her down to suggest a Natalie Duncan Appreciation Day or to throw her a parade. He'd come to…to…he wasn't entirely certain why he came. Revenge. Closure. Reconciliation.

The building loomed three stories tall. Due to the curtains, it looked to him like the top floor was a residence. A black iron fence surrounded the structure. It reminded him of an old time mercantile with the wares displayed on the porch.

Second hand store, my ass. She was a junk mogul. He got out of the rusty pickup truck he'd bought to get around town and approached the entrance warily. *It's not too late to turn tail and run.* Climbing the steps, he opened the front door, noting the vintage "open" sign clearly displayed in the window. A bell chimed above him. He held the door open for a smartly dressed woman who clutched fabric swatches and paint samples. Russ bobbed his head as she passed. She thanked him.

Inside was a large open space filled with vintage furniture, objects d'art, and architectural pieces. Antique doors were stacked in one area, corbels in another. An entire area was devoted to yard art. Advertising pieces hung on the walls, some framed, others not. There wasn't an inch of empty wall space anywhere. She had glass cases holding smalls—collectables and such. He was officially impressed. Not that he hadn't been impressed by her when he thought she owned some sort of thrift store catering to the indigent. He guessed she catered to interior decorators and designers. Peninsula was a haven for the wealthy, what with all the waterfront homes.

"Can I help you find something?" asked an attractive woman. She was dressed casual enough to climb on a stepladder and hang art, but stylish enough to wait on a wealthy collector on the hunt for a pricey treasure.

"Ah, yes." Russ cleared his throat, not entirely prepared for explaining his presence. "I just moved to town and I'm looking for some décor that would make my apartment feel more like home." His apartment needed a wrecking ball. He wondered if they had one lying about.

"What type of things are you interested in, Mr...."

"Crew." He extended his hand. "Please call me Russ." He detected zero recognition, confirming that Natalie probably didn't share the details of her hellish Christmas.

"I'm Lana." She shook his hand, displaying her

perfectly polished nails.

Natalie popped her head out from what appeared to be a back room, and then quickly vanished. The panicked look on her face gave him a small measure of satisfaction.

Smiling, he asked, "Are you by chance the owner?" Wouldn't surprise him if Natalie had lied about owning the shop on top of her other lies. But that *was* definitely her car parked in the carport.

"My sister is."

He wagged his finger at Lana. "I think I've met your sister. Natalie, right? Natalie Duncan." At least she hadn't given him a fake name. Hopefully.

Lana couldn't have looked more shocked if he'd dropped his drawers, bent over, and demanded she kiss his butt. "Right."

He planted his hands on his hip in a confrontational stance. He'd had enough of the fun and games. "Natalie! Come on out."

"How do you know Natalie?" her sister inquired, stealing a quick glance over her shoulder in the direction of the back room.

"Nat!" he called, confident the store was empty of customers. "Would you like me to tell your sister where I know you from?"

Natalie shoved the swinging door open that separated the showroom from the back area that said *employees only*. "Mr. Crew. What a pleasant surprise."

Dressed in black slacks, a fluffy cowl neck sweater, and chic pumps made for comfort as well as fashion, his anger melted away to attraction he hadn't anticipated. He'd sort of planned to give her what for. Seeing her, all he wanted to give her was whisker burn.

"I'm sure," he muttered.

She waved her hand in the direction of her sister. "I guess you've already met my sister." Turning to her sister, she shooed her away and said, "I can handle this, Lana."

Lana's eyes narrowed. "Aren't you Tiff's English teacher? Russell 'The Muscle' Crew? How do you two know each other?"

"I don't really care for the nickname," he said. He'd heard it circulating. It beat the nicknames he'd been stuck with in the past. Russ Screw, to list another. "It's not very inventive and doesn't even make sense."

The other part of her question he wasn't sure how to answer. He'd come to give Nat a piece of his mind. Maybe humiliate her a little. Make her feel really crappy about ditching him. But the way she looked and smelled flooded his senses with memories of how she tasted, how she felt in his arms. He didn't have it in him to hurt her. Much.

Lana gave him a head-to-toe assessment. "Makes perfect sense to me."

"Lana, please," Natalie said, her cheeks pinking up in what he hoped was embarrassment.

"Can we talk?" Russ glanced at Lana, still scanning him like he had a barcode. "Privately."

"Not a chance," Lana said. "What's going on here? Does it have something to do with Tiffany?" Lana grasped his arm. "Is she all right?"

"Tiffany is fine," Natalie said, bugging her eyes out at him. "Mr. Crew was just leaving."

He stared Natalie down while she avoided his eyes. "Your sister seduced me, then dumped me with a lie and phony phone number." Maybe he did have it in him to hurt her after all.

Natalie gasped.

"No. Freakin'. Way," Lana said. "My sister doesn't seduce people. If only."

Although that was comforting news, relieved that he wasn't one in a long line of men she'd warmed her bed with, he was still in pain. "Why, Nat? I'd just like to know why. You owe me that much."

"Yeah, why?" Lana echoed, turning her attention to Nat. "For the love of God, why?"

"Can we *not* talk about this right here, right now, please?" Natalie whispered.

"Where?" Russ asked. "When?" By the look on her face, he guessed the answers were *in your dreams* and *when pigs fly*.

"How 'bout tonight, my house, dinner. Then you two can duke it out," her sister said, including some air punches for affect.

"Lana!"

He crossed his arms over his chest. "I'm not eager to sit down and eat with her." Which was a lie. He'd not only eat with her, he'd volunteer to watch her eat while he starved. He'd eat off her.

"Don't you want us to hear your side of the story?" Lana asked. A blatant attempt to manipulate him, if he'd ever heard one.

"If he comes to dinner, I won't," Natalie squealed.

"Don't you want us to hear your side of the story?" Lana asked Natalie.

"I'll be there." Russ wasn't sure what made him say it. He had to see Natalie again, anytime, anywhere, under any circumstance. Plus, for some reason he didn't want her impugning his character to her family.

"Let me write down the address for you." Her sister hurried off, presumably to find a pen and paper.

With her hands folded over her chest, Natalie asked, "Why are you doing this, Russ?"

He pointed his finger at her. "I've been looking everywhere for you. I've called directory assistance, searched the internet, and drove to the damn ocean."

Her eyes grew wide in the face of his news. "I'm sorry."

"I'm pissed." He stabbed his finger at her. "I've been to every junk store, thrift shop, and antique emporium from here to the coast."

"I-I'm really sorry, but—"

"What makes me the angriest is that as mad as I am, I still want to take you in my arms and suffocate you with kisses." Thankfully he didn't actually take her in his arms and force his lips on her. Behavior like that reeked of desperation and could technically be interpreted as assault.

"Oh, my," Lana mumbled. She handed him the address. "Seven o'clock?"

He hated that he still felt so strongly about her to the point of obsession. Russ didn't know how to stop, didn't know if he wanted to stop. His stomach churned. She literally made him so sick he'd lost his appetite. The feelings he had for her actually hurt. It was a pain that made him feel alive. He wished he didn't feel quite so alive at the moment.

"See you then," he ground out between gritted teeth. Pointing his finger at Natalie again, he said, "Don't even think about blowing me off." He turned and stalked out of her store, the jingle of the bell above the door bid him goodbye even if Natalie didn't.

****

Natalie slipped in the back kitchen door of her sister's house where she found her eavesdropping by the doorway to the dining room. Shrugging out of her coat, Natalie draped it over a chair back. She shouldn't have come to Lana's stupid dinner party, but couldn't sit at home knowing Russ was spilling his guts to some of her nearest and dearest family. She had to keep him from talking at any cost. And honestly, she simply enjoyed looking at him.

She tiptoed closer. "Is he really here?"

Lana didn't even flinch, riveted to the action in the other room. "Oh, yeah."

"What nerve." She peeked around her baby sister to bask in the total hotness of Russ Crew. "Jerk."

"I dare you to say that a little louder." Her sister giggled.

Russ stood chatting with Clint—about guy stuff, if she had to guess. Sports. Porn. Prostate exams. Who knew what men discussed in semi-private? His face looked clean-shaven. His hair appeared freshly trimmed. She'd rather liked him scruffy, rubbing that stubble along her sensitive neck. Her skin throbbed in homage to the memory.

He wore faded jeans and a brown sweater pulled over a dress shirt. The collar poked out on one side like he dressed in a hurry. His stature was relaxed, holding a beer bottle in one hand. His other hand he used to gesture and emphasize the point of his conversation.

The two guys laughed about whatever he said. Hopefully not the harrowing couple of nights she'd spent stranded in that cabin with him. *How humiliating.* If the story got out, young men would cross the street to avoid her. Mothers would lock up their sons. Wives would lock up their husbands. The young ones, anyhow.

Glancing back at Natalie, Lana's perfectly groomed right eyebrow rose. "Don't you look extra nice tonight?"

"Do not." She was not one bit interested in hooking up with Russ Crew—again—but neither would she show up looking her age. She'd been meaning to try out that new wrinkle-reducing moisturizing cream before he ever stepped foot in her shop. It's never a bad idea to look your best.

"What's the story with you two?" Lana demanded for about the hundredth time that day.

"Nothing."

"It's a big, fat, whole lot of something." Natalie's sister strolled back to the stove. "There were accusations being flung around the store today amidst angry fireworks and a fog of sex appeal."

Natalie planted her hand on her hip, jutting it out. "He's crazy. Off his meds. Ought to be locked up for his own protection. And mine, too."

Lana eyed her skeptically.

"He's clearly a stalker," she whispered. "By his own admission, he's been hunting me down like prey." An image of him tracking her through the snowy woods, pouncing upon her and devouring her with his gorgeous mouth popped into her head and refused to pop out. "He threatened me with suffocation."

"Suffocation by kisses." Lana sprinkled some salt in her sauce. "You should be so lucky."

"Would you believe he's got multiple personality disorder and you've only seen the nice one?"

She shook her head. "No. I don't care what kind of disorder he's got. Did you get a look at his butt?" She made a squeezing gesture with her hands. She was a menace at male strip revues.

"I-I most certainly did not," she said, even though she'd not only seen his butt, she'd caressed it. Her nails had scratched red marks into that butt. "And by the way, thanks for putting me through this evening of hell on earth."

"You're welcome." Lana handed her a tray of crab-puffs. When Natalie was in high school she'd given her sister a bad perm. Lana said she'd get even one day, but really, this was extreme. The perm had relaxed after three months. "I hope he's not allergic to seafood. Is he?"

"I'm sure I don't know." Natalie crossed her arms over her chest, refusing the tray. "You don't seriously expect me to go out there and serve him, do you?"

"Are those crab-puffs?" Clint asked from the doorway. He crossed the room and gobbled a couple down nearly without chewing. "Try one of these, Russ. Oh, hey, hi, Natalie. You look nice tonight."

"Do not," she squeaked.

"Doesn't she look nice, Russ?" Clint babbled on. He reminded her of an exuberant puppy without the annoying piddling.

Russ trailed along behind Clint. Picking up a puff, Russ' eyes remained trained on Natalie. Her face heated up.

He popped the puff in his mouth. "Excellent," he said without commenting on her potential good looks. After all, he'd seen her at her worst.

"It's not like Spamghetti-Os," Natalie said, and

then pursed her lips.

Lana squared her shoulders. "What's that supposed to mean?"

Russ grinned. "Not much is like Spam and Spaghetti-Os."

Clint and Lana exchanged quizzical glances. "Let's eat," she said, probably afraid Russ and Natalie would fuse together and melt into a puddle of wet, sticky attraction on her tile floor. No amount of Mop and Glo would fix that sort of mess.

Natalie marched off to the dining room to face her fate. With a bowl of salad in one hand, an open bottle of wine in the other, she groaned low in her throat. While no one looked, she took a giant swig from the bottle she clutched by the neck. When everyone was seated, she filled her glass to the very rim before passing the wine to Lana who gave her a nasty look of derision. Wine was to be savored with sniffing, swishing and sipping, not chug-a-lugged, according to Lana.

After filling her glass half full, Lana asked, "Wine, Russ?"

He raised his beer bottle. "I'll just stick with beer if that's all right."

Natalie's eyes ping-ponged between the two. She knew it was not all right. Lana loved to throw dinner parties. She spent hours poring over magazines for the right color scheme, place settings, and centerpiece. Tonight's centerpiece was a bouquet of winter greenery interspersed with holly and flanked by green pine scented candles. Apparently nothing says, tell-me-all-the-raunchy-things-you-did-to-my-sister like the color green and the smell of pine.

Lana recorded every cooking show on TV, using

poor Clint as the guinea pig for her recipes before subjecting her dinner guests. A bachelor will go through great pains for a home cooked meal— something her sister knew quite well. She researched on the internet to make sure the wine went with the food, which went with the décor that complemented the occasion as well as the season. So, no, it wasn't okay for him to opt out of wine. If someone sat out of place, refused food due to an allergy or a diet, or God forbid passed on the wine, it threw Lana's world out of alignment.

She put on her hostess smile and said, "Suit yourself," through a clenched jaw.

Russ and Natalie sat directly across from each other. She concentrated on the oil painting of assorted flowers hanging on the wall behind his head. Impressionistic. Vibrant colors. Generous brush strokes. She'd price it at a couple hundred dollars in the shop. It really made his eyes pop. *Dammit!*

"Eggplant?" Lana passed Russ a platter of food, which thankfully for his continued good health, he accepted. "So, how long have you been teaching, Russ?" This was the polite dinner conversation portion of the evening. It wouldn't last.

"About four years," he replied, "if you don't count time served as a teaching assistant, but do count my first year as a substitute."

"He's a novelist," Natalie couldn't stop herself from saying. Why? She didn't know. If everyone was destined to discover she was a cougar, preying on younger men, she wanted them to know she had discerning taste. It's not like she pinched the butt of the bag-boy at the local supermarket, tucking a dollar bill into the waistband of his Fruit of the Looms. That was more Lana's style.

"Is that so?" Lana said with the perfect mixture of interest and awe.

"He's already landed himself an agent who's busy finding him a publisher," Clint added, albeit with a mouth full of food. A no-no at Lana's dinner parties. Clint should know better. And looked like he was going to try to get away with drinking beer instead of wine just because Russ did.

"An agent." Natalie's attention left the oil painting to meet Russ' gaze. "I didn't know that."

"I was just about to tell you when you left me by the side of the road like trash," he said, conversationally.

"In front of your apartment," she said in her own defense. Natalie couldn't be held responsible for the uncanny resemblance between his apartment building and a landfill.

"When I called you to give you the good news, I discovered you gave me a fake phone number, he said through gritted teeth.

"An innocent mistake," she said. Her excuse wouldn't fly since she'd also lied about where she lived and the name of her store. The lies of omission wouldn't help her case either.

Clint shook his head woefully back and forth. Lana made a tsk tsk sound.

Natalie rolled her eyes at the drama. "Okay, I'm sorry. Again. Still."

Connecting with her across the table, Russ said, "I wasn't sure whether to be worried or angry."

"I can see you settled on angry," she muttered.

"I never had you pegged as a cruel person until now," Clint said.

Natalie wanted to remind her brother how the entire affair was his fault for dispatching her to do *his* Christmas shopping. He owed her. But she didn't want to bring up the word affair in conjunction with Russ.

Raising one eyebrow, Lana added, "I never had you pegged as out-of-your-ever-loving-mind, or are you blind, Natalie?"

She felt a murder spree coming on. Starting with Clint for siding with Russ. Ending with Lana for siding against Natalie, with Russ in the middle because he'd been her one and only one-night stand. The term one-night stand dictated he go away, never to be seen again. Not follow her home and end up practically in her backyard. All of them together were painting her as a monster in this whacked-out picture, when nothing could be farther from the truth. It was called self-preservation. She didn't want to be forever remembered as the old broad dumped by the young hunk. Best to be the dumper.

Regardless of the illusion that she and Russ meshed very well both physically and intellectually, she was convinced they were mismatched. And she would not rest until she convinced him, too. Chemistry swirled in the air between them. That was a given, but Russ was destined to be a bestselling author, fated to marry the young starlet cast in the movie version of his novel. Natalie wouldn't even be a footnote in his memoirs.

"So, Russ," Lana said, "Tiff tells us your class is exploring the works of Hemmingway."

He nodded, his mouth full of food. He must have gotten the do-not-talk-with-food-in-your-mouth memo, or he had manners. After swallowing, he said, "'The Sun Also Rises'. One of my personal favorites. Then we'll move on to Mark Twain. In the spring—and I hope Tiffany will join my class in the spring—we'll be examining great women authors."

"Jane Austen," Lana said. As if she'd ever read Austen. "Tiffany is quite taken with you." She pointed her fork at him, which was also on her list of things not to do at one of her soirées. "I imagine all the young ladies in your class are charmed by you."

Natalie flung a cherry tomato at her sister, but she dodged it, having become adept at avoiding flying table food due to years of practice.

Russ bobbed his head. "They like me. I like them. I like the young men, too."

Clint cleared his throat. "Excuse me? What did you just say?"

"I enjoy young people," he confirmed. "That's why I went into teaching. I like to mold their minds and inspire their imaginations through literature."

"Oh." Clint returned to his food. "That's what I thought you meant."

"Tell us about you and Natalie," Lana said, eyelashes fluttering.

A jolt of alarm pumped through Natalie. She nearly choked on her salad, accidentally tipping her wine into the breadbasket, soaking the bread in crimson. "Oops." She mopped at the table with her napkin. *Smooth.*

Lana paid her little attention, returning her interest to Russ who was mid-chew again. He looked around the table after swallowing. Instead of recounting their passionate night of lovemaking, he drained his bottle and said, "Can I get another beer?"

"Of course." Lana made no move to replenish his drink. No one wanted to miss his response.

Rising from the table, he said, "Mind if I get it myself."

Natalie popped out of her seat. "I'll help you." She followed him to the kitchen, her hand squarely between his shoulder blades, prodding him along. "Why are you doing this to me? What could you possibly hope to accomplish?"

He opened the refrigerator. "I'm just trying to enjoy a nice, home-cooked meal."

"What do you want?" She threw her arms wildly, although kept her voice quiet. "Revenge? Sex? My tuna salad recipe?"

He spun around and said, "Yep."

Natalie rolled her eyes and groaned, not taking him seriously. "All right. Okay. If I sleep with you one more time will you go away then?" *Say yes to the sex and no to the going away.*

"Nope." He popped the top off the beer. "Not without that recipe."

"Seriously." She fisted her hands at her side. "What do you want?" *Please say me.*

He took a long gulp, pretending to ponder her question. His Adam's apple bobbed. "I'm holding out for an invitation to your sister's famous Valentine's Day Sweetheart movie marathon." He winked at her.

Natalie growled.

"After that is her annual St. Patties Day all-you-can-eat corn beef and cabbage feast." He rubbed his stomach. "Mother's Day brunch." Russ pursed his lips. "I can not wait to meet your mother, Nat. Hopefully I'll get an invite to the Fourth of July barbecue bash."

"No one," she whisper screamed, "wants to attend Lana's movie-freaking-marathon, Russ. People purposely leave town to avoid it. I ought to make you go just to watch you suffer through *Sleepless in Seattle*."

He spread his arms wide. "What? I'm having a great time. Clint and I are going to hit the boat show when it comes to town. And by the way, I love *Sleepless in Seattle*. Huge Meg Ryan fan."

She crossed her arms over her chest. "Good for you. Good for Clint. Good for Meg."

He tweaked her nose. "I like your sister, your brother, and your kid. Most of all, I like you. So sue me."

She decided he couldn't possibly like her. She'd been downright nasty. Clearly he was one of those guys who had to do the breaking up. He was punishing her for dumping him before he could dump her. "How many times do I have to say I'm sorry?"

"Forty-eight." He took a swig of his beer.

Her eyes narrowed at him. He'd come up with a number pretty quickly like he'd expected the question. "I know I'm going to regret asking, but why forty-eight?"

"That's roughly the number of hours we spent together. I'll give you credit for the three times you've already said it, so just forty-five more times. And you can't say them all at once, one right after the next." Russ walked away to the dining room.

"I'm going home now!" Natalie hollered from the kitchen. She'd be damned if she'd apologize forty-five more times. She stabbed her arms into her coat sleeves.

"The hell you are!" Lana yelled from the other

room. "Go on, Russ. You were just about to tell us about you and Natalie."

Lumbering back to the dining room, Natalie plopped down in her chair, defeated. Pouring what remained of the wine in her glass, she took a hearty drink.

"I'm sure Natalie recounted to you her adventure being snowed in," Russ said, taking way too much pleasure in her agony, if the lopsided grin on his face was any indication.

"Yeah," Clint replied, riveted to his words. "She's like a natural disaster magnet. Did Nat tell you the story of being stranded in a car with our folks during the eruption of Mount St. Helen's when she was just a baby?"

"Shut up, Clint," Natalie snapped.

"No." Russ turned to her. "She didn't."

"You should hear our mom tell the story." Lana touched his wrist. "Mom's convinced Natalie was scarred for life by the ordeal."

"Did Natalie tell you she was born during an earthquake?" Clint asked.

Eyeballing her, Russ said, "She failed to mention it."

"We don't like to talk about how she was conceived during a windstorm that caused a city-wide blackout," Lana added. "And then there was Duane."

"Enough, Lana!" Natalie barked. She didn't want the evening to end in tears. Her tears.

Russ shot Natalie with a penetrating stare.

She tensed, braced for Russ' tale. When recounting her version of events to her family she'd conveniently left out the part where she picked up a hitchhiker, sexed him up, and dumped him, leaving him with a fake phone number. *I had my reasons.*

"We were snowed in together," he said. "Me and Nat."

Lana touched her hand to his wrist again. "Go on." There was too much touching going on as far as Natalie was concerned.

"We used our body heat to stay warm," Natalie blurted. "Are you happy now? Is that enough information for you? Do we need to spell it out for you two? We did the nasty. We knocked boots. We bumped uglies. We did the horizontal mambo. He boned me."

"I was going to say I don't kiss and tell," Russ said. "But I like the way you tell it better."

Lana took Natalie's glass of wine. "You've had enough."

"That's got to be the most interesting how-did-you-meet story I've ever heard," Clint said to Russ. "Snowbound."

"More interesting than me and my first husband?" Lana objected.

"You met at a Rolling Stones concert," he said blankly.

Clint and Lana bickered across the dining room table while Russ and Natalie's eyes locked. Her head swam as she became lost in a sea of blue.

"Nat and I have to go," Russ announced, pushing away from the table.

"No," Lana whined. "We were going to play Pictionary. Games can give great insight into compatibility."

"Is that why you and your second husband always lost?" Clint asked. "We should play guys versus girls."

"Shut up, Clint," Lana said.

Natalie already knew she and Russ were compatible at the one thing she had on her mind. Rising from the table, she said, "We'll have to take a rain check."

Russ cupped her elbow, guiding her to the door.

Chapter Seven

Twenty minutes later Russ and Natalie sat parked around the corner from her house…or warehouse, as it were, making out in the cab of his truck like a couple of teenagers after a homecoming game.

"God, I missed you," he groaned between heated kisses. "I missed this." He cupped her breasts over the fabric of her blouse. "I missed these."

"They missed you, too," she murmured against his lips.

He gazed longingly at a glowing window of her house in the distance. "You've got to let me come up and…what did you call it? Do the nasty?"

She pulled away, her mouth hanging open in shock. "No. Absolutely not."

"We can call it whatever you'd like," he said. *Bumping uglies. Knocking boots. Horizontal mambo.*

"No." She grabbed his wrist, assessing his watch. "Tiffany will be home soon. You have to go before she sees us." Her lips smashed into his again, completely negating her statement. Russ was in no position to argue, his mouth being completely full of Natalie's tongue and all.

"Lunch tomorrow," he said when they broke apart.

Also in direct contradiction to her words, she straddled his lap, kissing him passionately. "We're incompatible." She combed her fingers through his hair.

"How do you know? We haven't even played Pictionary together."

He groaned when she wiggled and squirmed on his lap. He slipped off to a primal little corner of his mind where rational thought was not allowed. Only animal instinct.

"I'm wrong for you," Natalie said, right before she ran her tongue along his lower lip.

"You're so right." He'd resigned himself to the fact that there was no sense arguing with her. Not while she was fused against him, anyhow. "Let's meet tomorrow." *In my bed.* "And we'll break it off." *Eventually. Slowly. Or never.*

"Stop humoring me, Russ." Her fingers worked their way under his sweater and inside his shirt to caress his bare chest. "I want to be heard and taken serious."

He kneaded the flesh beneath her blouse. "We're incompatible. I'm wrong for you. I heard you."

"I'm wrong for *you*. You, you're perfect." She dived into his mouth.

Russ squeezed and caressed her curvy hips, pulling her tighter against him. "Right." He kissed her neck. "You're wrong for me." He tugged at her earlobe with his teeth. "What was I thinking?" His mouth claimed hers again. "So clear to me now."

She nipped and pecked at his lips, lingering against his for a leisurely exploration of his mouth by her tongue. Switching, he explored her mouth for a while.

"We can't see each other." She had untucked his shirt from the waistband of his jeans. "It's complicated."

"Complicated," he repeated. "Got it." His mind was too fogged with her fresh scent to manage anything more than repeating key words. His thumb dragged along the denim seam between her legs.

"That's not fair," she whispered, her body moving against his touch. "Not fair, not fair, not fair," she groaned into his ear.

"Call a cop."

With his free hand, he worked at the buttons of her blouse, planting his lips on the flesh spilling out of her bra. His finger dipped into the dainty lace, pushing the fabric aside to brush against her nipple.

"Russ," she hissed.

"Tell me what you really want, Nat. The truth."

Her fingers raked through his hair. She closed her eyes and bit at her bottom lip. Shaking her head. "I...I want you to...to...go away and leave me alone."

Stubborn to the end. "I don't think you do." He wondered if she really was scarred for life by the Mount St. Helens ordeal, or Duane like Lana said. *What happened to him?* Russ was afraid to ask. Helping her forget seemed like the best approach.

One handed, he flipped the snap of her jeans and eased down her zipper, the delicate sound boomed in the cab of his otherwise quiet truck. His other hand distracted her with feathery touches along the smooth lines of her ribcage, intermingled with powerful kneading in various fleshy areas—his favorite areas. Thighs. Butt. Breasts. He yanked her jeans down her hips a couple inches. His hand snaked into her waistband, cupping between her legs with his palm. He pressed and she moaned.

Natalie arched her back, tossing her head from side to side. "Oh, yes."

His touch grew firmer, more precise, pressing hard

between her legs, rubbing in a circular fashion. He sucked her nipple into his mouth, flicking his tongue against the hard tip. Her fingers dug into his shoulders, her body tensed. He had her physically where he wanted her, enslaved. If only he had her heart. His lips released the nipple to pursue her lips again. It was a good policy to keep her mouth busy kissing instead of talking, since he didn't usually agree with what she had to say. *Agreeing is overrated.*

Natalie rested her forehead against his, their ragged breath mingling together. "Yes," she mouthed against his lips, on the edge of a climax, if her heavy breathing was any indication. But he wasn't convinced it was the answer to his question. Merely an endorsement of his demanding touch.

"Have lunch with me tomorrow," he said, since she was in a yes sort of mood.

She shook her head and whimpered.

"Why not?"

"Because…because   you're   twenty-six   and I'm…I'm not," she stammered.

"So what?" *Dammit!* "Have lunch with me or I'll damn well stop."

"No!" She seized tight. Her body trembled and shuddered against him.

He held her, just held her until the moment passed. The last spasm of her climax took away his bargaining chip.

"Please. Please meet me tomorrow." He couldn't remain in the same town without her, especially knowing she lived so close. He couldn't look into her daughter's face every day. It was a younger version of Natalie.

She nodded an answer, giving in to his wishes and hopefully hers, too.

"I'll pick you up at twelve." He swept the hair from her face. "It'll be a long lunch. So plan accordingly."

Straightening her blouse, she said, "I'll meet you at your apartment."

Stubborn. "Fine."

****

Just as Russ predicted, it was indeed a long lunch that didn't involve food until about three o'clock when he ordered pizza to be delivered to his dingy studio apartment. They shared the pie in bed—naked.

He skimmed his fingers lightly over Natalie's sensitive skin, making her tremble with renewed need. "I see now what you meant last night about us being incompatible." He placed his lips on her bare shoulder, sending a pulse of energy shooting along her spine. "You are so wrong for me." A lazy grin washed over his face. Not just his mouth, the smile reached his twinkling blue eyes.

She lay on her stomach in his bed with her face nestled in her crossed arms. She traced her index finger over her wedding band circling his pinky finger, reflecting on the ring, her marriage, and how tragically it all ended. Natalie wondered how her life would have been different if…

"You want it back?" he asked.

She shook her head. "I thought I'd lost it forever. I know where it is. That's all that matters" He'd return it upon request. She had no worries in that regard.

"Good." He laced his fingers with hers. "I think of you every time I catch a glimpse of the ring, sick as that is."

She scoffed. "Sick?"

"The ring signifies your union to your dead husband. I've no right to wear it. I'm not even part of the equation."

"I feel free without it." Besides it fit him like it belonged on his finger. And she thought of him warmly every time she saw the ring on him. "I let myself be chained to the ring and everything it symbolized." Putting it back on might tether her again, or so she feared.

"I hope you enjoyed your taste of freedom." Russ nibbled at her neck. "Because you're taken now."

The smile remained on her lips, but sadness seeped into the darkest places of her mind. Losing her freedom, or what little freedom she had from Tiffany, terrified her. Would she become a slave to his whims? Tiff leaving the nest worried her, and at the same time intrigued her. *What am I afraid of?* Change, she decided. The unknown. Russ symbolized the hugest of unknowns. Would he compliment or complicate her life?

He must have picked up on her sudden change of mood, and said, "Don't worry, Natalie." His fingers tightened around hers. "I don't intend on chaining you in the basement. My fondness for you isn't intended to be a prison."

"No, I know." Her words rang hollow. She didn't even believe herself. She had a way of mothering everyone around her: Tiff, Lana, Clint, and Duane for a time.

Russ thankfully changed the subject. "About the ring, what's with all the initials engraved inside?"

"The ring has been passed down through my

family, starting with my great-great grandparents. Each couple engraved their initials and dates." Natalie snorted a laugh. "It's running out of room for any more."

His brow drew together endearingly. "Duane didn't give you the ring?"

"Oh, no. We were both barely eighteen. We didn't have any money. I dropped out of high school because of Tiffany. Duane was able to graduate with his class, but he went to work for his uncle in construction instead of his plan of heading for college."

"Stand up guy," he said.

"Yes." A tender memory of his simple proposal flashed in her mind. Poor guy hadn't much choice. But they had love and laughs. "Very much so. Eventually he opened his own window business."

"Ambitious," he added. Natalie heard admiration in his tone along with a hint of jealousy. Russ was at the beginning of his life's dream of writing. She kept forgetting he was young and possibly immature on some level. She kept forgetting because in most situations so far, he acted more mature than her.

"I suppose." She drew in a deep breath, letting it out slowly. "Or risky."

She was off to a dark place—the place where she'd start to reassess her incompatibility to Russ. Every time the glow of sex wore off she second-guessed her feelings and replaced them with guilt and doubt. She also sensed the conversation heading to the dreaded "how did he die" question. She didn't want...no, she couldn't go there without a fit of tears.

Needing to be in a state of euphoria—again—she said, "Make love to me."

"Happily." Russ started at her feet, kissing her instep. Caressing her calves, he loved her ankles with his lips, sending little pulses of pleasure surging through her entire body by way of an intricate network of nerves. She squirmed when he found a ticklish spot behind her knee joint. She buried her face in his pillow, muffling her laughter about his playful kisses on her thighs and butt.

Patting her bottom, he said, "Turn over."

Natalie flipped over. They'd been in such a frenzy earlier when she first arrived. They'd treated each other to a quickie. After a little nap, her desire for him had returned and they'd made love again—slower.

Settling into the mattress, she clutched the sheet to her breasts out of some outdated sense of modesty or unwarranted insecurity about her body. He pushed the sheet away a little at a time to kiss her abdomen, hips, and breasts. Especially her sensitive nipples, still erect from earlier, or erect again.

He swirled his tongue around her taut nipples—the right, and then the left. His lips trailed lower. His fingers lingered to gently massage her breasts. Her legs remained clamped shut until his kisses coaxed them apart. Natalie, fingering his hair, gasped when he swiped his tongue between her legs. The tender feathering of his hair by her fingers turned into raking at his scalp in no time at all. She hung on the edge of a cliff of desire and needed a life line. He matched her raking by boring his tongue into her until she clutched at the bed sheets instead of his hair. With his free hand, he pressed lightly on her abdomen, intensifying the storm of pleasure brewing in her belly. She dug her heels into the mattress. Warmth swirled and pooled in her belly like a whirlpool of sensual passion. Her thighs quaked and she cried out his name and rode the wave of the climax surging.

Seconds transitioned into minutes she could do nothing but breathe heavy and wait for her heart to return to normal. All she wanted to do was close her eyes and lose herself in sleep.

****

Natalie's cell phone chimed, waking Russ from a semi-slumber.

She reached across the bed. "Hello? Tiffany?" She pulled the sheet to her neck with her free hand. "I'm running errands."

He scoffed. *So now I'm an errand.*

She playfully punched him. He rolled out of bed and pulled on his jeans. He wasn't shy, but remained a little self-conscious about the scar on his hip, even though she had kissed it earlier. He crossed the room for a bottle of water and another piece of pizza.

She rolled onto her side, taking the sheet with her. "Make a salad or a sandwich." She closed her eyes and draped her arm over her eyes.

He guessed she was listening to a list of reasons Tiffany couldn't possibly make herself dinner. Dealing extensively with teenagers himself, he'd heard his fair share of excuses for a myriad of situations. Attendance. Homework. Tests. Kids had imagination, no doubt about it. They wouldn't need the excuses if they only put half the effort into their attendance, homework, and studying for tests as they put into their excuses.

Something about the conversation made Natalie sit up in bed, the sheet pooling around her waist. "You say you want to be treated like an adult. Adults make their own dinner." She collapsed against the bank of pillows in exasperation. "You know how to use the washer and dryer, Tiff. If not, you need to learn." She blew out a breath, making her hair billow up. "No. I'm not going to stop what I'm doing and rush home because your favorite blouse has a stain."

Russ couldn't help but laugh, silently. He'd had a few intellectual run-ins with Tiffany who was too-damn-smart-for-her-own-good. She could be very manipulative.

"There's some cash on my dresser, but don't take it all. Leave me some." Natalie flipped the phone over, dropping it on the mattress. "I think she hung up before I said don't take it all."

"Don't they always?" He offered a bite of his pizza.

She shook her head. "Am I a terrible mother?"

"Not even almost." He plopped down next to her. "Don't feel guilty, Nat. She's a big girl, a smart girl. Too smart, if that's possible."

"I know." She pulled the sheet up around her neck again. "I long for the good old days when I could outsmart her."

"Kindergarten?" He braced for her to clobber him with a pillow, but she didn't. She took his joke with a smile.

She fussed with her messy-from-sex hair. "Close enough."

"She'll graduate in a few months, go off to college, and then have her own life," he said. "Then it'll be about you and me." He waited for a protest, but she had refrained from too much more breakup talk. Mostly because he'd kept her mouth occupied from the moment she crossed the threshold.

"She'll always be my little girl, Russ."

"Right, I get that." He patted her leg. "You've done an amazing job with her. Tiffany is going to be a great asset in whatever she decides to do with her life. Because of you. You did that. You should be proud."

"Don't you want kids?" She bit at her lip, waiting for his answer. Waiting to pounce on another reason their relationship couldn't work. He wouldn't give her the satisfaction.

He shrugged. "I've never had that desperate need to procreate like some guys do."

"Me either, but you might. Some day." She sighed. "Tiffany was an accident, not that I regret one second of her—or Duane—that's not what I'm saying."

Duane. There he was again, the guy he had to live up to. Life after Duane had left her celibate for six years. The guy made him feel a little insecure. Was sex so bad with Duane she'd lost interest, or so great no one else stood a chance?

He'd never be sure if it was him who broke the ice around her heart, or was she just finally ready and he happened to be there with his thumb out for a ride. He'd heard women reach their sexual peak in their thirties. He had to hope what they shared was more than right-place-right-time. Mutual sexual attraction was a place to start and build from, but he wanted more from her. He wanted it all. She only needed to meet him halfway.

"You're awfully quiet," she said. "What are you thinking? Plotting your getaway, but you suddenly realized we're in your bed?"

"Nothing could be farther from my mind." He took a long drink of his water to wash away his doubts and fears. "But I am supposed to meet a group of students at the library, your daughter included."

"No wonder she wants to wear her favorite blouse." She shuddered. "My daughter has a crush on you and that's just weird, because I do too."

He smacked her bottom playfully.

"What was that for?" She smiled, clearly enjoying her stinging punishment.

"Your daughter doesn't have a crush on me. She thinks I'm older than dirt." *And that's okay with me.* He got the impression Tiffany looked at him the same way he looked at Mrs. Barberry, the geriatric girl's PE teacher. "I think she has a crush on a guy named Ronnie. He's taking engineering classes, if I'm not mistaken."

Natalie groaned. "I almost wish she'd have the crush on you."

"Are you fishing for another spanking?" He didn't need trouble like a mother/daughter tug-o-war over his attention. "I'm not getting a crush vibe from Tiffany."

"I was about her age when I started dating Duane," she said. "I was a lot like her, studious, a little socially awkward, immature for my age."

"So, basically just how you are now," he teased, blocking the pillow she chucked at him.

"Tiff thinks she knows everything."

His eyebrows shot up. "Again, just like you." He flinched, bracing for her to hit him again, but she didn't. Not that she didn't want to, if he had to guess.

"I don't want her to make the same mistakes I made. One in particular."

Russ stretched out on the bed, draping his arm and leg over her. "Natalie, they say life is short, but it's actually quite long. Over the course of her life, Tiffany will make mistakes. Same as you did. Same as I did. Everyone does. You can't stop it." Fine advice he didn't entirely buy into, but it sounded wise.

She pursed her lips. "If I locked her in her room I could."

He caressed her arm. "That seems impractical and borderline child abuse. My point is, you took your mistake and turned her into a triumph. Your mistake made you stronger. Your history made you the woman you are today. I like the woman you are today. And really, would you want to live in a world with no Tiffany?"

She shook her head. "Well, there was that one time when she was two and she pooped in the public pool."

Still caressing, he said, "She and Ronnie may decide they want to—"

Wincing, she said, "Bite your tongue!"

"Have you talked to her about sex?"

"How can I?" She threw her hands in the air. "She knows more than me."

"I hope not." He shook that notion from his head. Natalie was the total package in and out of bed. She oozed sex appeal and passion without even trying. She also oozed smarts and humor and so much more.

"She mocks me and laughs at me because she thinks I'm celibate"—she choked out a laugh—"which was true until recently."

"If she only knew the truth," he teased. He'd run out of sage advice. "Get the kid some birth control."

"Birth control!" She shoved him off her. "That's like an open invitation to do *it*."

"Why is doing *it* such a bad thing?" Russ got up

and paced around the room. He and Natalie did *it* and he'd never been happier. She seemed pleased as well. Or she had seemed pleased about five minutes earlier. "Why does sex have to equate to one person using the other person and one person being taken advantage of? There are worse things for kids to get involved in, Natalie. Drugs and alcohol just to name a couple."

Her eyes rolled back in her head. "Thanks, Russ. I feel so much better."

"All I'm saying is, from the dawn of time, women have been warned, threatened, and frightened into not giving up their virginity until marriage, or more recently, until they get a commitment." He sighed. "They say *I do* and suddenly they're supposed to open the floodgates of desire?" Russ tapped his index finger to his skull, which might have been taking his tirade one step too far. "It's too late, Nat. It's already ingrained in their minds that sex is bad for you...them. Sinful. Women battle that notion for the rest of their lives. Guys—we don't think that way."

"So you believe people should be fornicating all over the place, my daughter included?"

He wandered over to stand by the picture window overlooking the parking lot and dumpster. "No. I just think there's a double standard. If a guy gets a little...action, he's a rock star. If a girl does likewise, she's labeled a slut."

She chuckled, but it sounded fake. "Are you the voice of repressed women everywhere?"

He felt like it. She should be the one preaching to him about the inequality between men and women, not vice versa. "Society teaches girls to be prudes about premarital sex, but the perception follows some of them to the grave."

"Are you calling me a prude now?"

He turned to face her. "Without question." Case in point, he'd had to seduce her into agreeing to meet him and again once she arrived. She'd poised to spout her protests before she'd even stepped foot in his apartment. He'd seen it in her eyes. He'd thwarted her breakup nonsense right away by pushing all her sexual buttons until she peeled off her clothes and came to her senses.

Natalie threw back the sheet to stand naked in front of him. She stabbed her legs into her jeans before collecting her other articles of clothes strewn around the room.

"This is a perfect example." He threw his hands in the air. "We could start a pleasant discussion about the weather and you'd end up angry because you feel so bad about feeling good."

"What?" She yanked her sweater over her head, flipping her hair. "To be perfectly honest, it wasn't that good."

"Oh, ho, ho." He'd been word smacked. She was good, attacking his sexual skills. "That's not what you were saying about an hour ago. Or an hour before that."

She plopped down on the edge of the bed to pull on her boots. "I didn't want to hurt your feelings."

"*Then*," he added, "you didn't want to hurt my feelings *then*. Now—now that's all you want to do. I don't know if it's the widow thing, the mother thing, or the age thing, probably a combination. But this is exactly why you drove here today instead of letting me pick you up. You knew you'd be starting a fight with me and leaving in a snit." He glanced at his watch.

"Right on cue."

"That has absolutely nothing to do with why I drove my car," she said.

"Then why?" he asked. "Is it because you don't want your daughter or your sister or your brother, or God forbid, your neighbors to find out you're not a born-again virgin?"

Natalie gasped.

"It's obvious who's being used and taken advantage of in this scenario. Me." He turned his back to her. "You're the party doing the using."

"Poor, Russ," she said, "got a blowjob and some tail. What a tragedy."

"I got a snow job, Natalie." He planted his hands on either side of the window. "You've ditched me and lied to me. Now I'm an embarrassment to you. You've treated me like a dirty little secret. Does anyone even know where you are or who you're with?"

"No," she whispered.

"Thanks for being honest, at any rate." He glanced over his shoulder.

"I'm not embarrassed. Not in the way you think." She buried her face in her hands.

"If our roles were reversed, I'd be labeled a jerk of epic proportions for treating you so shabby."

Rubbing her temples, she said, "It's complicated."

"You're making it complicated." He pushed away from the window. "I'm planning our future and you're planning an exit strategy." He crossed the room to the bathroom, turning on the shower. "I've got to get ready to go. I promise not to bother you any more. You've got my number and you know where I live. Ball's in your court."

Russ wanted to slam the bathroom door between them, but couldn't shut the door in her face. Sitting there on his bed, she was obviously in pain at the thought of ending things. But he refused to continue meeting in the shadows while she denied him in public, for whatever archaic reason. Secretly he hoped she'd peel off her clothes again and join him in the shower.

Natalie stood. He waited for some protest, an apology, anything. She let out an exasperated breath and left, slamming the door. He flinched when her engine revved. He guessed she left a little rubber behind when she peeled out of the parking lot.

Chapter Eight

Russ scoped out a quiet corner of the library that had a grouping of six comfortable chairs. Plopping his book bag down next to a wingback, he ran his fingers through his hair. His quarrel earlier with Natalie left him on edge, grinding his teeth, and no doubt glowering a bit. But he owed his students his undivided attention. He couldn't let his personal life interfere with his career. Been there. Done that.

Some of the more voracious readers had expressed an interest in meeting outside class, and he personally invited some failing students to join them, hoping one group might help him help the other group. Positive peer pressure.

Tiffany showed up a couple minutes early, which meant Ronnie would make an appearance as well. The little redhead, Felicity, trailed in within seconds of Tiffany, scooting her club chair close to Russ. He'd sort of hoped for a few minutes to bond with Tiffany before the others arrived. Why, he wasn't certain. His relationship with her mother stood on shaky ground. He ended up with eight students in all. Not a bad turnout. The last to show sat cross-legged on the floor. They discussed the goals and agenda for the evening.

He arranged ahead of time for the librarian to give them a quick orientation of the library. He followed that with a lively discussion about Hemmingway that went on longer than he anticipated due to questions and answers. After which time he set them loose to explore the wealth of literature while he graded papers.

Russ could have left, but he dreaded returning to the scene of the argument. His apartment was a blight on his otherwise nice neighborhood. Noisy. Cold. Impersonal. Besides, the kids made the effort to show up. He owed them his time in exchange for their effort. A library was like a second home to him anyhow. His apartment barely qualified as a first home.

Felicity sauntered over asking innocuous questions to which she already knew the answers. She hung on his every word, laughing at his less than witty replies. She was transparent in her motives, showing up early for class each day, calling and emailing questions about homework, and hanging back after class each day. The redhead dominated class discussions with inane babble. Russ wanted to shake her to her senses. She was a smart girl acting dumb to gain his attention.

By nine o'clock, all who remained were Tiffany, Felicity, and Ronnie, who wouldn't leave until Tiffany did.

All four filed out into the chilled night air. The temperature, along with small clumps of snow that clung to the ground, reminded Russ of Natalie and the cabin they'd shared. He smiled remembering their snowball fight. He frowned recalling their recent verbal battle.

"Can I get a ride home, Mr. Crew?" Felicity asked. "My roommate dropped me earlier and borrowed my car for the night."

A story he doubted. He shouldn't put himself in such a compromising situation. Her request had "bad idea" written all over it. Also a bad idea leaving her stranded without a ride home. He'd never forgive himself if something happened to her. But on the bright side, a ride in his old pickup would probably cure her infatuation. Russ noticed Ronnie and Tiffany leaning against his Camaro, deeply embroiled in conversation.

"Ronnie!" Russ shouted, complete with a wave of his hand. "Are you giving Tiffany a ride home?" Without waiting for an answer, he added, "Maybe you could take Felicity, too."

"Absolutely!" he replied, enthusiastically. "We can make a Ronnie sandwich."

"Eeuw!" Felicity exclaimed. Tiffany punctuated Felicity's "eeuw" with a gasp. Russ halfway expected her gasp to be followed by a slap across the kid's face.

Russ flung open the passenger door of his truck. "Tiffany! Get in." He motioned to Felicity. "You, too."

While the two girls complied, he crossed the courtyard in long, powerful strides toward Ronnie, who got a worried look in his eyes.

Backing toward his car, Ronnie said, "It was just a joke, Mr. Crew."

Russ put his hand on the boy's shoulder, grasping tight. Tighter than he intended, feeling too protective over Natalie's daughter. "Can I give you some advice, son?" Ronnie nodded his reply. "You'll get more action if you treat girls with respect." He was not qualified to give advice. He had no clue about women.

Still nodding, Ronnie said, "Yes, sir."

"But not that girl." He pointed at Tiffany, who sat poised along with Felicity, watching the exchange from the cab of his truck. They could speculate about his words from his actions, but Russ and Ronnie were far out of earshot. "She's just shy of seventeen."

"Jailbait?" The kid's voice shot up an octave.

"That's right, son."

"But...but she's in college," he protested.

Russ slung his arm around Ronnie's shoulder. "Nevertheless, she's sixteen. But she might be worth waiting for."

Ronnie nodded. He appeared numb as if someone sucker punched him in the gut. Waiting months, possibly as much as a year for a girl was a tall order for a college guy. To the ears of a young man, the task no doubt sounded harder than scaling Everest. Another worthwhile endeavor.

"Have a good night, Ronnie." Russ slapped him on the back and returned to his truck. He slid behind the wheel. "Where to, Felicity?"

She waved her hand dismissively. "Why don't you take Tiffany home first?"

Nice try. He turned the key in the ignition. The truck rumbled to life. The smell of exhaust filled the cab. "Felicity, where do you live?" *Or prepare to hoof it.*

She remained quiet for a few beats, probably considering her only other option would be as an open-faced Ronnie sandwich, since the guy still stood next to his car in shock. Felicity folded her arms over her chest. "On Bunker. Straight ahead. Left at the light."

Russ pulled away from the curb. Minutes later he deposited the redhead in front of her building in a puddle of disappointment. He idled the truck, waiting for her to enter the building and vanish from sight before he headed to Tiffany's side of town.

"I live on Vine," she said. Good thing she had,

otherwise her suspicion would have been raised if he'd found his way to her house without directions. "Do you know where that is?"

He nodded. "That's a pretty blouse, by the way." He wasn't sure if it was the same blouse that needed Natalie's expert washing and ironing earlier in the day. He didn't see a stubborn stain.

She glanced down. "Thanks."

Silence encased them in an uncomfortable bubble. *I shouldn't have mentioned the blouse.* Russ had ripped her from the clutches of the guy she'd been crushing on, he'd insisted on dropping Felicity first, and then he complimented her appearance. The last thing he needed was his girlfriend's daughter thinking he was attracted to her. Hopefully Natalie was still his girlfriend, if she ever had been. Although, the word girlfriend trivialized what he felt for her.

"I'm so embarrassed about what Ronnie said," Tiffany whispered. "He's such a jerk."

"He acted like a jerk," Russ agreed. "There is a distinction. Consider giving him a second chance. Maybe a three strikes policy."

She shrugged like she'd consider it. "I think Felicity likes you...you know...too much."

Glancing at her, he watched the glow of a streetlight cut a path across her face. "She's confused."

"Is it against the rules for you to date her?"

Some colleges frowned on teachers dating students. Other schools banned the practice. "It is, but even if it wasn't, it would be wrong."

"Why?" Tiffany tilted her head. "She's an adult." The way she said adult led Russ to believe Tiffany held the title in high regard.

"Because I'm in a position of authority over her. It would be inappropriate. Do you understand?"

She shrugged. "I guess."

He wasn't sure if she understood or not, but she was a smart girl. Smart enough to peg Ronnie's remark as embarrassing and disrespectful, bordering on insulting. "I'm way too old for her. And I'm not interested in her."

Tiffany pointed. "I live right here."

He stopped at the curb alongside the warehouse that doubled as a home. "See you in class, Tiff."

She snorted a laugh, reminding him so much of Natalie. "That's what my mom calls me." Opening the door, she said, "Thanks for the ride."

"Anytime," he said. "I mean that Tiffany. Anytime."

"I know."

"Don't get in a car with a jerk or a drunk. Call your mom, or…or call me. I'm serious. Even if you're drunk yourself, or worse."

She assessed him through questioning eyes. "Okay."

He cleared his throat. "Don't forget to read through chapter twelve."

She stood rooted in place. "Mr. Crew, would you like to come in for a cup of coffee or something?" She looked at him through a veil of pity, which was better than fear over his odd behavior. Or worse yet, infatuation.

"Uh…" Natalie would kill him, which made the offer tempting. He'd love to see the look on her face. Oh, hell, he'd love to see her face. The last thing he wanted to do was return to his dreary apartment. The only redeeming quality was that his pillow might hold her scent. "I better not."

"My mom's home. I'm not trying to jump your bones," Tiffany said with one of those "as if" scoffs. "I talk about you all the time. I know she'd like to interrogate you about my grades, my friends, my manners, followed by listing the reasons I'm too young to be attending college. Needless to say, she *loves* meeting teachers." Tiffany dragged out the word loves like it had four or five syllables. "Anytime. Anywhere. For any reason. It's what she lives for."

I doubt that. "Unannounced?"

Her eyes rolled. "She keeps the house white-glove-inspection-ready."

Eyeing the third floor window where light filtered out from behind sheer curtains, he said, "Sure." *Why not?* "I'd love to meet your mom."

Tiffany led him up the back steps, chattering the entire way about class, her classmates, and college next year. "I hope Mom's not doing something embarrassing like watching her favorite Bon Jovi concert DVD in her jammies, eating ice cream out of the container, stopping only to sing into her spoon as if it were a microphone."

Russ sort of hoped she was. He chuckled at the image Tiffany planted in his brain.

"Mom!" she called.

"In here!" Natalie called back, shooting a jolt of anticipation tearing through Russ like a bolt of lightning. He recalled their afternoon tryst fondly, reliving the highlights, ignoring the fight like it never happened.

Tiffany dropped her backpack on the wood floor, hung her coat on a peg, and ventured further into the house. She stopped suddenly, turned and slapped her hands to her cheeks in mock horror. "Oh, God. I hear Bon Jovi."

"I hope she saved us some ice cream," he said.

"Unlikely, Mr. Crew."

He followed her down a long hall. The white walls were adorned with black and white photos of Tiffany at various ages and locations, hair in pigtails, covered in mud, asleep. Natalie was in a few of the pictures, along with a man. *Duane.* Russ slowed to take in the gallery of photos. Curiosity prodded him along. Duane was a nice looking guy with dishwater blond hair, a smiling face, and laughing eyes.

They passed several closed doors before the space opened up into a loft area with high ceilings and massive pillars for support and aesthetics. The front of the loft had a large picture window with a much better view than his apartment. She'd decorated with found objects of years past. Chippy painted shutters lined the windows as art, along with an antique screen door to nowhere. Framed pieces of sheet music, vintage movie posters, and antique memorabilia hung from the walls that had much in common with her store below. No empty space.

Natalie sat on an overstuffed couch, slipcovered in a floral fabric. Assorted throw pillows were scattered about. She typed on her laptop keyboard. Stacks of paper covered the old steamer trunk she used as a coffee table. He guessed she was catching up on her bookkeeping or the like.

Tiffany waved her hand in his direction. "Mom, this is Mr. Crew."

Natalie looked up from her work, a pair of reading

glasses perched on her nose. She wasn't in her pajamas, but looked plenty casual in jeans and an oversized sweater that revealed a hint of one shoulder, no bra strap in sight. Her hair was piled on her head, held with a clip. She looked radiant, like a woman getting plenty of sex.

"Is that Bon Jovi I hear?"

Tiffany laughed at their private joke. "Mr. Crew gave me a ride home from the library."

An awkward silence followed. "She was protecting me from an infatuated student," he admitted, maybe to make her a little jealous. "Nice place. I'm in awe. It's not what you expect from the outside." Actually, he expected nothing less than amazing from Natalie, who sat there looking at him like he had a third eye.

"When I get my own place," Tiffany said, "I'm going to get normal stuff. Mom? Are you okay?"

"Yeah." She took off her glasses with one hand and reached out to shake his hand with the other. "Nice to meet you, Mr. Crew."

He took her hand. "Please, call me Russ." Their eyes connected and locked. He wondered if she'd showered away the remnants of their lovemaking, or did his sweat and saliva still coat her skin? "Your daughter is my star pupil. A real delight." He kept shaking her hand, not telling her anything he hadn't already shared. "I wish they could all be like her."

"My mother will take all the credit," Tiffany said, lightheartedly. "Mom, you're freaking me out. Honestly, Mr. Crew, I've never seen her this quiet."

Natalie dropped his hand like he'd given her the mother of all static shocks.

He slid his hands in his jean's pockets and rocked

on his heels. "Did you say something about coffee, Tiffany?"

"Yeah." She shook off her curiosity. "I'll make a pot."

"Decaf," Natalie said, absently. Once her daughter was out of sight, she whispered, "What are you doing here?"

Russ didn't sense anger. More like fear. Fear that Tiffany would discover she was a mere mortal instead of Supermom. An image of Natalie baking a cake, while simultaneously checking Tiffany's homework, and ironing a pile of freshly laundered clothes, flashed through his mind. Not only did she bring home the bacon, she fried it up in the pan. Looking around, he decided she made it all look easy and chic.

"I didn't plan this," he protested. "She insisted." *Sort of.* That was the story he was sticking to. It would be his word against Tiffany's. "Can we talk somewhere private? Or would that be too obvious?"

Natalie got up from the couch and peeked into the kitchen. She grabbed a jacket from a coat rack in the corner. "Tiff, I'm going to show Mr. Crew the view."

"Okay. I'll check my email while the coffee brews."

Natalie waved him over to a spiral staircase that stretched toward the ceiling. He admired her bottom the entire climb.

"Wow," Russ muttered, a little intimidated by the sunroom they ended up in. It was nearly all windows on four sides with a three hundred and sixty degree view. Lush plants grew in clay pots. The room reminded him of an oasis in a desert. Two lounge chairs rested on one side, a bistro table on the other. Despite the season, the space felt warm.

"This is where I spend my staycations," she said. With one hand, she opened a door leading to the roof, while flipping a light switch with the other hand. A whimsical string of white twinkle lights lit the outdoors.

He followed her onto the flat torch-down roof that spanned the entire warehouse. The patio was every bit as charming as the loft, decorated and furnished with a creative eye. But it was the view that took his breath away. Mountains loomed in one direction, topped with snow, surrounded by clouds and lit by the moon. Another direction showcased a peek-a-boo view of the waters of the Puget Sound. The city lights glowed in a third direction. A neighboring house took up the fourth direction, not as inspiring.

He breathed a deep, cool breath of air, letting it fill his lungs. Blowing out the breath, he said, "Duane left you pretty well off."

Russ realized how she must see him. Young and poor. A wannabe author teaching literature part time because those who can't do—teach. He wasn't good for much except in the sack. He was surprised she let him make love to her in his crappy apartment on sheets he'd bought at a discount store. Maybe she thought he was in the market for a sugar-mama.

"Duane left me grief-stricken, broke, and desperate. His death was…unexpected to say the least." Her cold breath clung in the night air, visible for a few seconds before vanishing. "He thought…we thought we had time." Her voice cracked. "We had this run-down warehouse with his business on the first floor. Storage on the second floor. He was mid-renovation when he…he passed. We were living in two rooms while the rest was gutted. We had no life insurance, no health insurance. And I had a little girl to look after. Everything you see, I made happen."

"I'm sorry, Nat. I don't know why that should surprise me." He felt like a shit. "You amaze me."

Natalie rubbed her hands together. "With help from my family and friends, we slowly fixed the place up. My brother Clint was a godsend. To get by, I sold everything on eBay, starting with Duane's tools. And having yard sales every weekend because I couldn't find a fulltime job."

"It snowballed from there." He recalled her words. Put into context, they made more sense now.

She gripped her hands around the ledge that surrounded the roof. Moisture glistened in her eyes. He bit back the question of how Duane died, fearing she'd break down and weep. A blotchy face and puffy eyes would be hard to explain to Tiffany.

Russ placed his hand over hers. He half expected her to shake off his advance. After the fight they'd had, he wasn't sure where he stood with her. She was an independent woman. He liked that about her. He also longed to be needed by her. For more than sex.

"I think your daughter forgot about us."

"She doesn't forget about much and nothing gets by her. I'm sorry about this afternoon."

He shrugged. "We both have strong opinions. I just need to keep mine to myself."

"Maybe we could agree to disagree"—her hand folded into his—"especially where my daughter is concerned."

He decided not to share the Ronnie story. Maybe in twenty or thirty years she'd be ready to hear it. Even though Russ was sort of the hero of the story. He'd protected Tiffany's honor or virtue despite their earlier argument when he'd claimed he didn't believe in such things. And he'd intervened with no thought of Natalie. He found himself feeling instinctively paternal when it came to Tiffany.

"I have her best interests at heart whether you and I are an item or not," he said. "I hope you realize that."

"I do."

"Where do we go from here?" Might as well get right to the point. *I want to be with you.*

"I don't know, Russ." Her admission sounded painful to admit. "You were right. I've been on my own for so long, being an overprotective mother. Before that a wife. Add our age difference, our other differences, my hang ups." She looked up at the stars as if wishing for a miracle. "And then there is your theory about us gals protecting our long-gone virginity."

"Please, don't pay any attention to me." He should have kept his big mouth shut. Russ accused her of picking the fight. In reality, it might have been him goading her, testing her. "I should save it for my writing."

"No." Natalie turned away from the night skies, returning her attention to him. "If we can't talk to each other, why waste our time?"

He slid his hand behind her neck, rubbing gently. "We're not wasting our time. I'm sure of that."

"Russ, when I left your apartment today, I went straight back to the shop and I told my sister about us. Point blank."

He stopped rubbing. "You did?"

She blinked up at him several times. "Yes, you

were right."

"I was?"

Closing her eyes and shaking her head, she said, "But I just can't bring myself to tell Tiffany. She'll hate me if I date her college professor, especially after I was so staunchly against her participating in this college program. She'll think I'm sabotaging her." She sighed. "Can I call you that? Her professor? It sounds so sexy."

"Sure." *Yes. Please.* He was more of a teacher or instructor than a professor. He didn't understand the allure of the word professor, but where Natalie was concerned, he was all for it.

"She'll never forgive me." Her voice cracked. "Never accept you. Us."

He pulled her close, kissing her temple. "Let me take care of it."

"Coffee is ready!" Tiffany shouted from somewhere in the house, her declaration muffled by the time it reached the roof.

Natalie pulled away.

"Trust me?" he asked her.

She nodded, unconvinced. He followed her into the sunroom and down the stairs. The aroma of coffee mixed with the scent of potpourri and old wood. However pleasant the smell, all he wanted to do was bury his face in her hair and drink in the fresh bouquet of her hair and skin.

Chapter Nine

Natalie couldn't believe Russ was in her house. His presence felt surreal, like a fantasy gone renegade, leaving her lightheaded and weak. Even stranger was Tiffany serving them coffee in the living room from Natalie's good decorative pot with the matching sugar bowl and cream pitcher. They were mostly for show.

"Who are you and what have you done with my daughter?" she asked.

Tiffany rolled her eyes. "Can I see you for a moment in the kitchen, Mom?"

How is it teenagers have the ability to enunciate every single letter in the word mom like it has three syllables, yet they can carry on an entire conversation via text message in four letters?

She glanced at Russ. He shrugged. She followed Tiff into the kitchen. Had she somehow found out her mother and teacher knew each other? Knew each other very well. Maybe Tiffany spotted them talking intimately on the roof earlier. She didn't see how. Maybe the attraction she and Russ shared made them glow or flash neon like a road sign or worse. A noxious odor or something.

Striking a defensive pose, Natalie asked, "What did I do?" *And why do I sound like the teenager?*

"Nothing." Tiffany opened a cupboard and reached for a plate. She stacked cookies on the dish like freaking Prince Harry was stopping by for tea. "Mom, I think Mr. Crew is really lonely," she whispered. "He's not from around here, so be nice to him."

"I'm nice." *Holy guacamole!* She'd been super nice to him. Many times.

"Some days he's so sad." Tiffany shoved the cookies at her mother.

"Did he say so?" That didn't sound like the man she knew, sharing his feelings with students.

"He hides it well," she said, somberly. "But I can tell."

Natalie shut her eyes and shook her head. Tiffany, the drama queen had them living in their own personal reality show. She took the plate of cookies Tiffany forced on her, reminiscent of the day before when Lana had also demanded she *serve* him. "Really? How can you tell?"

"I just can." Her face appeared so severe that Natalie couldn't possibly take her serious. "I'm very intuitive."

"Really?"

"Yes. Everyone says so. Would you just pretend to like him, please?" Not only did Tiff's words plead with her mother, her eyes sought a little solidarity as well. "For a few minutes? Act interested in what the man has to say. Just until he reaches the bottom of his coffee cup?"

She held her free hand up in surrender. "I'll do my best."

When they returned, Russ sat sipping his coffee. "Should I go?" he asked. "I'm probably keeping you up."

"We're night owls," Tiffany said. "Have one of my

mom's homemade chocolate chip cookies."

"Don't mind if I do." He plucked one off the plate Natalie held out on the palm of her hand like a butler. She crossed her eyes and shook her head for his benefit. Apparently he couldn't fight off a grin, although he appeared to try valiantly.

Tiffany was indeed a night owl, as advertised. She also seemed to be off her rocker. Natalie routinely went to bed by ten o'clock, rising at six. Where was this nonsense coming from and why?

"How is Tiff doing in class?" she asked Russ, although he'd already told her.

"Mom!"

"A, so far," he replied. "A plus probably."

"Told you so," Tiffany said, a self-satisfied smirk on her face. "But enough about me, why don't you come over Saturday night for dinner, Mr. Crew?"

Russ and Natalie locked eyes in confusion. She shrugged covertly, making it appear more like a nervous tick. If she didn't know better, she'd think her daughter was trying to fix her up. The first time she'd attempted a date after Duane's death, her daughter had a major meltdown. If she'd been two instead of twelve, Natalie would have characterized it as a tantrum. The last time she dared date again, which was also the second attempt, Tiffany came down with the flu. That was three years ago.

Narrowing her eyes in her daughter's direction, she said, "I'll ask again, who are you? And do I have anything to say about this?"

"I'll bet it's been a while since Mr. Crew has had a home cooked meal," Tiffany said. Turning to Russ, she asked almost like a dare for him to deny it, "Am I right?"

"You are right." He nibbled the cookie, seemingly enjoying himself too much.

Natalie knew for a fact it hadn't been that terribly long, although he hadn't actually finished his meal at Lana's house. Fate intervened, or her and Russ' desire for each other had. Hunger is hunger. She wondered if Lana or Clint had mentioned the disastrous dinner to Tiffany, even though she'd later sworn them to secrecy.

"My mom makes a great lasagna," Tiffany added. "You'd love it."

"You mean you love it," Natalie muttered. Clearly she had no idea the work that went into the dish. She made it from scratch and it took nearly all day. "But...yeah...I mean sure. I could make lasagna." She wouldn't mind showing off her culinary talent to him.

"I really wish I could, Tiffany," he said. "Natalie, I appreciate the offer. But I've got a faculty thing this Saturday. I'd much rather have dinner here...with you two, but I'm sort of obligated. I hope I can get a rain check."

"Faculty thing?" Tiffany said. "What kind of faculty thing?"

"Tiffany, really," Natalie said, astounded by her impertinence. Her daughter hadn't gone to such lengths to embarrass her since the shoplifting incident in the fifth grade. "That's Mr. Crew's business." *But, yeah, what faculty thing?*

"Please, call me Russ. Both of you." He snagged a second cookie off the plate. "I don't mind, really." He actually seemed uncomfortable with the title of Mr. Crew. "It's some sort of lame Christmas party."

"It's January?" Natalie pointed out. Maybe he'd

suddenly decided she wasn't worth the bother. He could at least come up with a better story than a Christmas party. He owed her that. Maybe this was payback for ditching him with a fake phone number by rejecting her with a phony engagement.

"Tell me something I don't know." He took a sip of coffee. "I'm the one who has to go *alone* to a belated Christmas party with folks I don't know, all because school isn't in session over Christmas. What's worse is there's a certain science teacher, who shall remain nameless, with the hots for me. And I'll be trapped in a buffet line with her breathing down my neck."

"Sounds awful." Natalie exaggerated a shiver. Although it really did sound awful.

"It gets worse," he said. "There will be dancing. What if—"

"Take my mom," Tiffany said.

"What?" Natalie clutched her chest. If Tiffany was getting an A plus, why was she offering her own mother up like a bribe? Or was she meant to be some sort of punishment for an imagined transgression?

"Please, Mr. Crew. Russ. You'd be doing me a favor," Tiffany said. "She seriously needs to get out more. Get back on that horse. And she'll totally throw down with the science teacher."

Natalie opened her mouth to protest, but she might actually engage in some sort of fisticuffs if the alleged science teacher put the moves on Russ. That was no lie. She wouldn't win, but she'd go down fighting.

"You should see my mom in a little black dress. No one, and I mean no one loves a buffet like her," Tiffany said, and Natalie couldn't deny that truth. "And she can salsa like nobody's business."

"Salsa?" He tilted his head in one of those you've-been-holding-out-on-me poses.

"It was a phase," she whispered. She'd gone through a slew of phases over the years. Candle making. Flower arranging. Scrapbooking. All in an attempt at fulfillment, or something similar. A poor distraction from sex maybe. "I don't want to talk about it." *Or do it.*

"You had me at the throw down with the science teacher." He tried valiantly to hide a smile she saw shinning in his blue eyes. "I'd be grateful if you'd agree to go with me, Mrs. Duncan. Natalie." He waited a beat. "What do you say?"

Tiffany blinked several times, a nervous tick from her childhood. "Mom?"

"If you think it will help save you from the unrequited affection of the science teacher, then sure." *Well played, Mr. Crew.*

The telephone rang and Tiffany dashed off to answer it like a well-trained dog at dinnertime.

"It's too late for phone calls!" Natalie called. Turning her attention back to him, she asked, "What just happened?"

"I have no idea. I figured you had some kind of mother/daughter mind control over her."

She rolled her eyes. "I wish." They stared into each other's eyes for a few seconds. She wasn't sure what he thought. She wanted to melt into a kiss that would involve several body parts and last until daybreak. "I'll walk you out." That seemed prudent.

He pushed up to standing. "It's going to be agony not to be able to kiss you goodnight." So he had been essentially thinking along the same line as her.

They walked outside. He followed her down the back stairs to his truck. His hands were shoved deep in his pockets like cuffs, keeping him from ravaging her like she wanted to be ravaged. Natalie sort of wished she owned the key to set his hands free.

"Is there really a faculty Christmas party Saturday night?" *Please, God, no.* "Or was that just a really bad lie? It's not wise to lie to Tiffany. She can smell deception a mile away. She says it smells like chicken."

"I wouldn't lie about something potentially that boring." He offered his hand to shake. "I think she's watching us, otherwise I'd shove you up against my truck and do some serious damage to your girl-next-door reputation."

A zing of desire ricocheted around her body, settling between her legs. "It wouldn't surprise me…about her watching us, that is." Natalie cleared her throat. "But why? What's going on?"

"Who cares about the why?" Still holding her hand, Russ rubbed his thumb along her knuckles. "How can she object to us dating now that she put us together?"

"Brilliant, Mr. Crew. You have her convinced you're sad and lonely. Apparently I'm the cure. Go figure."

"I *am* sad and lonely," he said, allowing Natalie her hand back. "I was lonely before you arrived up at my house today, and then again after you left. I guess it showed."

She shook her head slowly back and forth.

"It's late and cold." He tweaked her nose. "I do not want you sick come date night. There will be no second-guessing, no backing out, bailing out, or freaking out. Understood?"

She snapped to attention and saluted him. "Yes, sir."

"Can I please have your real cell phone number now?" he asked.

****

For the next forty-eight hours, Natalie fought a primal urge to be with Russ. Instead she spoke with him via the phone frequently and covertly to ease her pain and his, too, from the sound of his angsty pleas to meet in secret. She found the idea of a clandestine encounter exhilarating, but feared the possible backlash if caught by Tiffany.

The slamming of an automobile door lit a sexual fuse in Natalie that sizzled a path down her spine, landing and exploding in her lower belly. She dashed to the window, heart pounding in anticipation. Watching Russ stroll from his truck toward her house rocked her insides.

"How do I look?" she asked Tiffany as she drifted by with the phone to her ear.

Her daughter rolled her eyes. "My mom's having first date doubts," she said into the phone. "You look fine. It's only a dumb faculty snorefest. You'll be home in a couple hours."

The doorbell rang. Natalie squeaked a surprised exclamation even though she expected him. "Get that, Tiff." She shooed her toward the door.

"Jeez, Mom." She shook her head. "It's only Mr. Crew. He's seen you looking much worse."

You have no idea.

Tiffany opened the door, the phone still to her ear. She vacantly waved him in, pointing her mother out before wandering away to her bedroom.

He looked at ease in a casual suit, no tie, like he wasn't trying nearly as hard as her. And why should he? The man looked good in anything, everything, or nothing at all.

He motioned toward the door with a bob of his head. "Shall we go?"

She nodded, grabbing her wrap and purse. "Am I overdressed?" She thought it appropriate to wear the little black dress, as promised, so he wouldn't have any buyer's remorse.

"No, I'm underdressed as usual. I don't own a tie," he said, with a shrug. Probably a lie just to be nice. He pulled the door closed behind them, stopping to nuzzle her neck now they were alone. "You're my best accessory. Gorgeous."

His words did nothing to calm the erratic beating of her heart. If anything, his endearment had the opposite effect. His fingers skimmed along her lower back, tracing the path of her zipper, lighting another fuse of desire.

Heading for the truck, guiding her with a respectable grasp of her elbow, he asked, "Do you mind if we take the truck? I know it's not glamorous, but…"

"It's fine." She had fond memories of the truck. Not the least of which was the smell of oil and wood and him. His truck had bounced her around the other night like some sort of foreplay before he'd satisfied her passion for him right there at the curb. *Yep! I like the truck.*

He opened the passenger door, simultaneously glancing up to the third floor windows.

"Is she watching?" she asked. For all her daughter's recrimination about it being nothing but a boring faculty mixer, Tiffany acted as if she had a lot riding on this date. More so than her mother.

Russ waved up to the window. "She sure is," he mumbled through a smile, securing the door behind Natalie.

Looking around the cab, she noticed he'd done some cleaning. No more trash covered the floorboards or dash. The odor of motor oil and wood and Russ mixed with pine scented cleaning supplies. He confidently rounded the front of the truck to the driver's side. Once behind the wheel, he flashed her an easy smile before turning over the ignition. The heap of metal rumbled to life. He put it in gear and pulled away, leaving her house in the rearview mirror.

Two blocks later, he eased to the curb, letting the truck idle. "Come here, you."

She melted into his embrace. They exchanged a proper kiss.

"I would have brought you flowers," he said between pecks, "but I thought that would look too much like a date to Tiffany."

"Better to keep things casual for now," she said, although she'd love a bouquet of flowers to display in the privacy of her bedroom where she could admire them without Tiffany making a fuss.

"Let's you and I make quick work of this soiree and go back to my place." He punctuated his idea with a sensuous kiss on her neck, followed by nibbling her ear lobe, ending with her lips again.

She tilted her head. "So you just assume I'll sleep with you tonight?"

"Yep."

She narrowed one eye at him. "We'll see."

"You don't have to sleep if you don't want," he said, with a sly wink.

After a kiss to his chin, she said, "I don't have to do anything I don't want to do." That's what she'd learned from years of living on her own without a man. She believed her statement a little less in his presence. Russ Crew made her do things she'd never done before. And like it.

"Baby," he murmured, "how could you not want to be ravaged after a faculty Christmas party in January?" Pecking at her lips, he added, "I heard there'll be mini-quiches. Cheap red wine will be served up by clumsy students subsidizing their meager incomes. Peninsula College Jazz ensemble will be providing holiday music."

She pressed her lips to his, if for no other reason than to shut him up. "I'm ready to run screaming in the opposite direction."

"I know." He rested his hand on the steering wheel. "I'd rather be snowed in again." He kissed her temple. "Only with you, of course."

"Yeah, next time let's take provisions and stay snowed in until spring."

He chuckled. "Sounds like a plan."

Russ put the truck in gear and pulled onto the dark, deserted residential street. They traveled the few blocks to campus. After he found a parking space, Natalie slid across the bench seat behind him.

"I would have come around to open your door," he said.

He draped his arm over her shoulder in a blanket of calming warmth. Why she felt so nervous was a bit of a mystery. True they were on their first official date and she hadn't dated since—forever. But her naked body was on a first name basis with his naked body. They should be beyond jitters. This was a test. Would people stare and talk? There might be some finger pointing. Would there be gossip later?

His hand slid down to the curve of her waist and he pulled her tight against him. "This is fun, so far."

Because all they'd done *so far* was kiss in the semi-privacy of his truck. "Fun," she repeated. Pushing through the doors of the student center, she decided the night would be like a teeth cleaning. Not painful. But uncomfortable. And with food, music, and a Christmas tree. No laughing gas to dull the senses, just wine.

"I don't know too many people," he said. "Let's find someplace to sit."

She pointed to a table on the fringe of the activity, located near the back where the light shone dim. Russ pulled her along through the crowd of people as the band played *Frosty the Snowman.* It didn't sound bad. They put a snazzy spin to the song, making it their own. Too bad Natalie was long tired of holiday music that started in November with an implied promise to end at the New Year.

Russ hung his jacket on the back of an empty chair. Taking her purse and wrap, he placed both on the chair next to his and offered her his hand to dance just as the ensemble transitioned nicely to *Santa Baby.*

"I'm not intoxicated yet," she said. "But the night is young."

"Come on, Nat." He bolstered her confidence by covertly blowing a kiss. "We've done this before."

"In a cold, dark cabin while held hostage by a blizzard," she said. "Not under these extreme

172

conditions." Trapped, hungry, dirty dancing had nothing on shimmying in front of an audience of his peers.

He led her to the dance floor. A foot-stomping scene crossed her mind, but she wanted to avoid scrutiny. Being remembered as the new guy's elderly date dogged her hard.

Russ pulled her close. "I think it's safe to say we're the best looking couple here." He kissed the tip of her nose. "I have you to thank."

She noticed he didn't say they were the youngest couple. For some reason, she felt quite old. Looking around the dance floor, she said, "Some of these people look too young to be teachers."

"It's a party for all college employees. Accounting. Clerical. Cafeteria." Russ dipped her. "Hey, are you hungry? I'm starving."

"Of course. Sure." She hadn't eaten all day, hoping she'd look svelte in her dress. And she'd do nearly anything to end the dancing.

He spun her around. "Let's hit the buffet. Then we can hit the sheets." He waggled his eyebrows at her.

She couldn't help but smile at his exuberance. She looped her arms around his neck. "I don't feel respected as a person when you talk like that, Mr. Crew."

Nuzzling her neck, he replied, "I respect the hell out of you. I'd like to respect your brains out. Soon."

She giggled. "First, let me rescue you from this infatuated science teacher of yours. You point her out; I'll make sure she knows you're taken."

"I made that up," he admitted. "I have a student I'd like to ditch though."

She chuckled. "I could ground her."

The song ended, only to be followed by a jazzy rendition of *Jingle Bells*. Russ guided her away from the dance floor with his hand on the small of her back. They made their way to the buffet line, and then back to the table.

"The food's pretty good." She'd anticipated rubbery textured food, tasting bland. Buffets tended to serve the warm food cold and the cold food warm. Everything looked and smelled good. For a small college, Peninsula had a fine reputation.

Russ sipped ice water. "The Culinary Arts Department made it as part of their grade."

He waved occasionally at people, mostly students. He introduced her to a few other faculty members, and together, she and Russ danced a couple more times.

Finally he turned to her with desperation reflecting in his eyes. "Can we go now?"

She sighed. "I thought you'd never ask."

Slinging his arm over her shoulder, he pulled her close and they made their way to the exit. He waved across the room to people and shook a couple hands on the way out. He seemed pretty popular with his students and his peers. She guessed he'd been popular in high school and college, too. Natalie had been average, and then pregnant. His popularity aside, Russ breathed his version of a heavy sigh of relief once they were outside.

"Would you like to see my classroom?" he asked. "Or rather it's mine for one hour a day."

"I'd love to."

****

A short walk and five minutes later, Russ turned the key in the lock, pushed open the door, and flipped on the lights. "Well, this is it." He stepped aside for

Natalie to enter. He'd remembered the space being more impressive the first time he saw it.

She nodded, spinning around to take in the entire room. "Very nice."

"Like a classroom."

"Very much like a classroom," she said. "Where does Tiffany sit?"

"Right up front. Third seat from the left. Would you like to see my office? It's not so much my office as is it Mr. Ballantine's, but he's in England studying the great works of Shakespeare. Probably studying a pint of ale from what I hear. But it's mine until the end of the term." He couldn't stop himself from pointing out his unimportance.

"Sure."

He switched off the lights and locked up. He took her hand, leading her down the corridor, past the vending machines and the custodian's closet to the dead end that was his temporary office. On second thought, he decided her opinion of him might hit rock bottom due to the crappy location, combined with the size and general appearance of his windowless office that wasn't even his office.

When they reached his door, there was a note wedged in the crack of the frame.

"What do we have here?" he wondered out loud. He wrestled the door open with the key while giving a fraction of attention to the note. "She strikes again."

"Who?"

"Felicity," he muttered, ruefully. "A student. She must have grown tired of leaving messages on my phone and email." Russ was entitled to a private life. The school and students didn't own him. At least she hadn't tracked him down at his apartment.

"Is that the student you're trying to shake?"

He nodded and flipped on the desk lamp. He read the concern in her eyes despite his casual words and demeanor. A young, pretty student was vying for his attention and he didn't know how to completely express to Natalie that he couldn't be less interested in the girl if he tried.

She snatched the note from his hand, perusing the words. "It's not crossing any line."

The girl hadn't offered to have his baby or be his sex slave, but she'd become a nuisance. Unless his imagination ran amuck. "No, she keeps it class related, so far." He tossed his keys in a dish on his desk. "She just gives me *the* vibe."

Her head tilted. "The vibe?"

He'd mentioned this vibe to her before. Either she was oblivious to the vibe, or no one had ever pinged her with a vibe. He found that hard to believe, guessing she'd had several admirers over the years whether she'd realized it or not.

"You know, the 'I'm trouble' vibe." He shut the office door behind them. "Like I'm going to regret the day she signed up for my class."

"Oh. The vibe. I met a guy at my gym like that." She exaggerated a shuddered. "Clingy. Talkative. Inquisitive. He plucked imaginary lint from my shirt. Talked to my breasts instead of my face. Creepy."

A flash of jealousy washed over him. Taking her wrap and laying it over a chair back, he asked, "What did you do to get rid of him? I'd appreciate any suggestions."

She shrugged. "I stopped exercising."

"Interesting remedy." He enveloped her in an embrace. "Let's not let *her* ruin our evening."

Natalie pecked at his lips. "What did you have in mind, Mr. Crew?"

No further discussion ensued about what they'd do next. His intense kisses answered her inquiry. She didn't object. He didn't need to say anything else. Natalie clung to him like Saran Wrap. She hiked her leg against his good hip and he slid his hand up her thigh until her stockings ended and her bare flesh began. He pressed her against the office door, pinning her in place with his body.

With his knuckles, he stroked the panel of her panties and she moaned. "These panties have got to go."

Lowering her leg, she wiggled out of the lingerie, handing them over to Russ. He stuffed them in his back pocket. She planted her foot on the seat of the chair next to the door and slowly raised her dress like a curtain on opening night. Her flesh was the headliner.

He let out a breath. "Someone got a bikini wax."

"I've been dying to show it to you," she said, breathlessly.

"I'm glad you waited until now." Russ ran his fingers along her outstretched thigh.

Natalie gasped at his intimate touch.

She hadn't wanted mini quiches, dancing, or punch. She'd been hungry for him. This was what she'd craved all night long, being in his arms, tasting his kisses. He'd awakened something in her. Something insatiable. Natalie was starved for his touch and his tongue and... She'd had six years of drought to make up for. But Russ was more than merely a second string replacement for her husband. He was the real deal. Her future. If she'd let him be more than an instrument of pleasure.

She worked at unfastening his slacks while he worked her flesh into a heated fervor beneath his hands and lips. Standing there in his office, they joined in passion that couldn't be contained or postponed for a more appropriate location. Or perhaps the setting intensified her desire due to fear of discovery.

A flash of heat burst in her lower belly like striking a match. The warmth spread, sweeping lower until the fire exploded. He didn't stop.

Her legs wavered in her heels. She sank against the door waiting for her body to finish quaking and her breathing and heart rate to slow. Russ groaned into the curve of her neck. The tremors in her body began again, like an aftershock in the wake of an earthquake. Natalie bit her lip to keep from crying out. Against the door they held each other, their breath mingling.

With time came awareness and mobility. His hands cradled her head, his lips peppering her face with kisses.

She caressed his cheek. His arms and torso. She traced the raised scar on his hip. Now would be an ideal time for him to tell her how he'd come by the scar. She had a feeling the tale somehow involved his ex-girlfriend. "What time is it?"

He looked toward the clock on the wall and squinted in the dim light. "Almost eleven."

I need to get going.

Russ pulled out with a guttural grunt and fastened his slacks while Natalie adjusted her dress.

"I'll never think of this office the same way again,"

he said, a smile in his voice.

"Let's not share with Mr. Ballantine, or he won't either."

"Mr. B. and I don't have that type of relationship," he said. "Actually we don't have any relationship at all."

She could make out his laptop on the desk. A printer rested next to the computer and reams of paper. "How's the book coming along?" Somehow she braved that question, but lacked the courage to ask about his scar and limp. His writing was a safe subject. If he wanted to share his history with her, he would. She guessed he didn't want to any more than she wanted to recount her husband's death.

Russ pursed his lips. "Good."

Cupping his jaw, bringing his eyes to hers, she said, "You'll have to do better than that."

"It has a beginning, a middle, and an end. I'm just layering, editing, proofreading."

She tempted him with a kiss meant to coax more information. "When can I read the rest?"

"It's not Christmas, Mrs. Duncan."

"Tell that to those knuckleheads you work for. Seriously though, I want to read it."

"Soon," he promised, with a peck on her nose. "My agent thinks some things should be cut and other stuff needs to be expanded on. I want you to read it at its best."

She sighed. "I should get home."

His arms tightened around her. "Not yet. Let's go back to my apartment. Just to watch TV...or talk. We can go for coffee or something."

"Things were simpler back at the cabin," she said.

He feathered her arm with his fingers. "The cabin...now that was paradise. You know, except for being cold and hungry."

"Wet and dirty." Burrowing into him, she added, "Especially dirty."

"Spend Sunday with me. Just you and me."

She pulled away, retreating from his warmth and love. "I can't, Russ. The second Sunday of each month I go to the swap meet out at the county fairgrounds." She had to keep a roof over their heads and food in her and Tiffany's bellies. Not that they were in immediate danger of being homeless. Far from it. Those days were over. But potential poverty never stopped haunting her. Instead of food and shelter, she worried about college tuition and dorm fees.

"I love a good swap meet." He waggled his eyebrows playfully.

She scoffed. "Admit it. You've never been to a swap meet."

"I've never been to a Christmas party in January either. I wouldn't have missed it for the world. And I have a truck. Imagine all the crap...I mean treasures we could haul home."

Natalie fantasized about all the large, heavy pieces she could buy with Russ to help her haul them. Her hand wrapped around his bicep.

"I could be your junk hero." He flexed the muscle she clutched to persuade her.

"Impressive," she said. "Okay."

Chapter Ten

Russ showed up bright and early Sunday morning as directed. Natalie had said she wanted to be at the swap meet when the doors opened. The sign on the window to her shop said closed, but the door opened when he turned the knob. The bell chimed. Lights glowed in the predawn hours.

"Hello," he called.

"Russ," Lana greeted him warmly. "You don't know how happy I am to see you again."

"Good to see you, too." *Unexpected.* He'd envisioned a private, early morning tour of the store and maybe some necking with Natalie in dark corners. "How's Clint?"

"Fine. Fine. Natalie will be ready soon." She linked her arm through his. "So tell me all about this book you're writing. We didn't get a chance to talk much about it the other night at dinner. Is it dirty?"

He cleared his throat. "Not really." *Gritty and dark maybe.* She wouldn't want to hear that.

She wrinkled her nose the same way Natalie sometimes did. "So, I wouldn't like it?"

"Um...not sure." Lana wasn't easily put into any one certain demographic. "I hope you will."

"Enough about that," she whispered. "Tell me about you and my sister. A little birdie told me you two went out. Where did you go? What did you do? How did it end?"

"I better not," he whispered back. "I feel like I'm on perpetual thin ice with Nat." One wrong word could be his last.

Lana waved her hand in annoyance. "Aren't we all?"

Natalie materialized from the back room of the store wearing jeans, a festive sweater, and sensible walking shoes. When she entered, Lana dropped Russ' arm like she'd been zapped by a Taser.

She shook her head. "Stop pestering him, Lana."

"I'm just trying to see what kind of lunatic…I mean," Lana cleared her throat, "man would volunteer to go junking with you. He looks sane to the untrained eye." She narrowed her gaze at him.

"Junking?" he repeated.

Natalie snorted a laugh. "And you're a good judge of sanity?"

Her sister shrugged off the insult. He had a feeling they'd been trading barbs for years.

Russ did a cursory assessment of the store, noting the large size of many of the pieces. His hand absently reached back and skimmed his vertebrae. He'd once been an avid bicyclist until he had a cycle versus automobile incident. He went up in the air like a pop fly on game day, coming down more like a brick to the hood of the vehicle that hit him. His hip bore the scar from the ordeal, but his back would sadly never be the same.

Natalie used her thumb to smooth out the wrinkle that had formed between his eyes. "Stop worrying."

"Lift with your knees." Lana demonstrated.

"Oh stop it," Natalie said. "He volunteered for

this." Sounded to him like she said *he had it coming.*
"Russ?" She turned to him. "Do you have rope?"

"Rope. Check," he replied.

Arching an eyebrow at him, she asked, "A tarp?"

"Tarp. Check." Although the weather was dry and cold. So far.

She smiled, looping her arm through his and led him to the door, but it felt like she might be leading him to permanent disability.

"Have fun." Her sister waved.

What have I gotten myself into? He'd wanted to spend more time with Natalie, but in retrospect, he may not have thought this through. He'd pictured them walking hand-in-hand through the swap meet, picking up a few small to medium sized items. Making out in the parking lot. Maybe stopping for lunch on the way back. A spontaneous detour to his apartment on the way home for a quickie, if he were lucky.

All in all, it wasn't a bad day. He enjoyed her company on the drive as she chatted nonstop about reclaimed items, pointing out architecturally significant houses to him, and of course they talked about her favorite subject—Tiffany. Natalie treated him to a bacon double cheeseburger at the concession area so he'd potentially have the strength to tote her purchases. By all accounts her rationale made sense.

Mostly, she made the day fun, encouraging him to look at books. She asked his manly opinion about pieces she pondered buying. He guessed she didn't actually consider his opinion, but he appreciated being asked all the same. He was amazed by her eye for items others might deem garbage. Russ found that the sellers where pretty eager to help him cart off their discarded treasures in order to be rid of them.

Natalie would muse about turning electric insulators into candleholders, old chairs into planters or birdbaths, and anything able to be framed—old greeting cards, sheet music, calendars—was potential art. She had regular clients who had her on the lookout for collectibles from sports memorabilia to nautical pieces to glassware. She snapped photos and emailed them to the buyers. By the time they were done, she had made more in sales than she spent. And making sales made her very happy, extremely loving, and incredibly affectionate. He imagined that when he finally made a literary sale, he'd be equally happy and twice as affectionate.

Russ nuzzled her neck in the cab of the truck before they got back on the road with her purchases. "Come home with me," he said, against her neck.

Natalie shook her head. "Can't. Tiffany." Her hand clasped the back of his neck, holding him to her. "You could...you could come home with me. I'll make you dinner."

He tugged on her earlobe playfully with his teeth. "Spam?"

"Not Spam." Her words breezed by his ear in a whisper. "You have to behave yourself in front of Tiff though."

He caressed her shoulder, skimming down the length of her arm. "Therein lies the problem." He peppered soft kisses along the curve of her neck. "But I'll give it a shot."

"Promise?"

When it came to Natalie, he seemed to lack self-control. Touching her was imperative, like breathing. If she wasn't with him, she wasn't far from his thoughts, like a string around his finger for remembrance. Only her string wound around his heart several times, tangled, twisted, and was tied with a stubborn double knot.

He rested against the seat of the truck in resignation. "I promise to try to behave."

****

After unloading her purchases, Natalie pushed through the door of her home with Russ on her heels. Antiquing always left her in a rush of excitement, followed closely by exhaustion. "Anybody here? Tiffany!"

Russ placed his hand on her back, sliding his palm up her spine to her neck. He encircled her waist with his arm and weaved his fingers into her hair, holding her firm while he kissed the back of her neck. She swatted him away. He chuckled.

"In my room!" Tiffany called.

He pulled Natalie into his arms and kissed her lips while the coast was still clear. She struggled halfheartedly, enjoying the attention and the danger of potential discovery. She acted more teenagerish— tempting fate—than her daughter.

Several blissful seconds passed before they broke apart. "Stop it." Something she should have said sooner if she didn't enjoy his childishness so much.

"I'll behave"—he glanced at his watch— "starting…right…now."

Tiffany came out of her bedroom at the far end of the hall. "Oh, hi, Mr. Crew."

He rocked on his heels, hands stuffed in his pockets. "Hello, Tiffany."

"I invited Mr. Crew to join us for dinner." Natalie's face felt flushed with heat. "How about a nice chicken salad?"

He patted his stomach. "Sounds good. I'm still stuffed from that bacon double cheese burger, but I'll make room."

"Oh, no." Tiffany groaned. "It's Sunday. She didn't drag you to the swap meet, did she?"

"She did."

"And bribe your compliance with a greasy burger?" she asked.

"Yep."

"And you're still here?" Tiffany asked in a droning tone, denoting her disdain for all things swap meet related. As a child she had often been carted to the swap meet. The happiest day of her life was probably when Natalie declared her old enough to stay home alone. "What are you—a glutton for punishment?"

"I am," he said proudly like he ought to be entitled to a merit badge for suffering.

Tiffany scoffed, apparently agreeing. "You deserve a medal."

"I deserve a parade or a party. At the very least, a plaque, but I'll settle for dinner." He wore an exaggerated frown for Tiffany's benefit.

Natalie rolled her eyes. She didn't care to be the butt of everyone's jokes, but was happy Russ and Tiffany got along, as did Lana and Russ. And Clint and Russ. The common glue bonding everyone was all of *them* teasing *her*.

"How about a board game while we wait for the grub?" Tiffany headed to the living room without waiting for a reply. Granted, she was accustomed to getting her own way. *I blame myself.*

Sometimes Natalie regretted having only one child, robbing her daughter of a little brother or sister to play with, share with, learn to negotiate. She'd never have what Natalie had with Lana and Clint. It never seemed like the right time to have another child. No time. Not enough money. Then it was too late for her and Duane. And immaculate conception didn't seem to be a real thing.

"You're on." Russ followed Tiffany into the living room.

Natalie trailed after them. Tiffany opened the steamer trunk they used as a coffee table, digging through the contents, making a mess. Natalie bit her tongue. *Pick your battles.*

"I'll have her eating out of my hand," he leaned in and whispered.

She crinkled her nose. "Good luck with that."

Parting ways, she headed to the kitchen, leaving him to partake in a death match board game. Because that's the way Tiffany rolled. Dice that is. Everything was win or lose, do or die. *I don't know where she gets that.* Natalie listened to them laugh, talking about people from school she didn't know while she chopped celery and onions for the salad. She carried them each a soda, fighting the impulse to run her fingertips over Russ' broad shoulders.

He glanced up from the game. "Do you need help?"

She smiled and shook her head, returning to the kitchen. It was enough that he entertained Tiffany, or that she entertained him.

"Mom's in her element when she's got the

opportunity to feed people," Tiffany muttered under her breath, like feeding others was a crime punishable by firing squad.

"Nurturing is an admirable quality," he said, his defense of her reputation making her smile. "You are a very lucky girl, Tiff."

Tiffany's eyes darted to Natalie in the open kitchen. They exchanged an understanding glance. "I know." The admission sounded like it pained her.

It was strange to hear. She knew Tiffany appreciated her, but the words were usually left unsaid. Her daughter had become her world, eclipsing everything else—that was all coming to an end. She'd go off to college, making new friends, developing new interests. Maybe Tiff would fall in love or have her heart broken. This was the time in her life when Natalie was supposed to reconnect with her spouse, but she had none. They would be free to explore undiscovered hobbies and travel the globe while her daughter forged her own path through life if Natalie did her job of parenting right.

She carried out the tray of food to the living room so the game could continue. Normally she insisted on eating at the table, family style. Small family style. She wanted Tiffany to go to college, meet a guy above her economic station, and be able to impress him and his family with some good table manners and social graces. She also wanted her to get an education and be able to take care of herself. She wanted her daughter to have options that she never had. Not that Natalie would have chosen a different path.

Picking at her salad, Tiffany asked nonchalantly, "So…are you two like dating or something?"

In unison and without hesitation, Russ replied *yes*, Natalie declared a fervent *no*.

Tiffany looked from one to the other. "Would you care for some time to get your stories straight?"

"We're…you know…just two people engaging in planned activities in an effort to get to know one another better…for…for the sake of platonic companionship," Natalie explained, nearly choking on the word platonic.

Russ and Tiffany connected across the coffee table and both said, "Dating." They both laughed.

"We're friends," she said. *Good friends. Best friends. Friends with benefits.*

"Jeez, I hope so, Mom." Tiffany nailed her with one of those *you're too lame to live* looks. "Dating enemies is a bad idea."

She noticed Russ staying way outside the line of fire, instead he scarfed down his chicken salad, despite his earlier claim of being stuffed.

"Whatever," Natalie said.

"Whatever," Tiffany echoed.

Her daughter seemed unaffected by the fact her mother and her teacher may or may not be dating. The board game and her dinner were clearly a priority. Natalie wondered how she'd react if there was hand holding and kissing involved in this alleged dating. What would she do if her mother spent the night at her teacher's place? She doubted anyone would call Child Protective Services. She shook the image from her mind.

Russ lightly touched her arm with his fingertips. "Are you okay, Nat?"

She nodded rather unconvincingly and picked at

her food.

Standing, he announced his intensions of going home. His plate was empty. Tiffany had him against the ropes as far as the board game went. Going home seemed like a better option than being obliterated by a teenager, she guessed. Who could blame him?

"No," Tiffany said. "Stay." She forced a smile. "I'll get the dishes. You two"—she collected the plates, eyeballing them both—"get to know each other better." She ended on an eye roll before turning and leaving.

Natalie mimicked her eye roll with one of her own. Russ plopped back on the sofa a little closer to her than earlier. She could hear the water running and the clanking of dishes.

Taking her hand, he said, "I think she likes me."

Natalie cringed when a plate crashed to the floor. "Us dating should cure her of that."

"I got it!" Tiffany shouted.

"That's her being passive aggressive," she whispered. She'd been around the block with her teenage daughter and understood her moods, her tactics, and she recognized retaliation when it shattered against the kitchen floor. Tiffany knew how much she loved her Fiesta Ware.

"Come on," he said, "you must have dated some."

She gnawed at her lip. "Once when she was at summer camp." *Disaster. Don't get me started on the tantrum date that never was, or the vomit date that never was.*

"I'm jealous." He twirled a lock of her hair around his finger.

"Don't be."

Tiffany cleared her throat, almost like a warning

before she fully emerged from the kitchen, giving Russ a chance to disengage his finger from Natalie's hair. "Dishes are in the dishwasher. I'm going to go check my email. You kids don't do anything I wouldn't do."

They waited until Tiffany disappeared behind her bedroom door before colliding spontaneously together. Natalie draped her leg over his lap. He tangled his fingers in her hair. Their tongues intertwined in a rhythmic, primal dance of desire.

"Oh, gross!" Tiffany exclaimed.

Natalie and Russ peeled themselves apart. It wasn't easy. Sort of like peeling twenty-six-year old wallpaper off a thirty-five year old wall. Natalie wiped her soggy lips on the back of her hand.

Tiffany grabbed her purse, groaned and retreated back to her bedroom. The door closed soundly. Music blared.

"Shit," Natalie said under her breath. "Do you think she suspects?"

"What?" He tilted his head. "That you're human?"

"No. That we're...you know—"

Head still tilted, he arched one brow. "Dating?"

Pushing away from him, she said, "I think maybe you should go."

He pulled her closer again, but she planted her hand squarely against his firm chest. "When can I see you again?" he asked.

Relaxing in his arms, she feathered her fingers through his hair at his temples. "Barring any unforeseen circumstances," *like tantrums and vomit,* "Tiffany is going to a slumber party this weekend."

"A slumber party?" He chuckled. "I keep forgetting she's a kid. In class she acts like she's thirty."

Natalie kissed his chin. "We can have the house to ourselves." And she wouldn't have to be made love to in his dismal apartment. She kissed his cheek. "You can spend the night. All night."

"I gotta see you before next weekend."

"We will," she said.

****

Russ jotted some key points of his lecture on the dry erase board, enjoying the smell of the markers for some odd reason. The scent reminded him of words and debate and learning.

He regularly arrived to class early. He didn't like to write while he talked. When he spoke to the class about literature, he wanted an exchange of ideas. His hands were his instruments, like a conductor. The words on the board kept him on task; otherwise the lecture could go off in some other direction. Not always a bad thing.

With his back to the door, he heard it swing open. Looking over his shoulder, Russ froze, surprised to see Dr. Cunningham, the president of the college. He'd expected Felicity, his early bird come to help pass out handouts and play twenty questions.

"Don't stop what you're doing," he said. "Looks like an inspired lecture."

"Hope so." He finished out his list of bullet points and turned to the administrator. "What can I do for you, Dr. Cunningham?"

It wasn't often the president of the school dropped by. Actually it wasn't *ever* that he dropped by. He hadn't had much interaction with the man since joining the staff. Russ was a part-timer and more than likely a short timer. His goal had been to fly under the radar, avoiding any drama or workplace politics.

"You're due a little one-on-one," the older man said. Russ pegged him at late fifties to early sixties. The guy seemed well liked by all. "I've heard good things from the other instructors and students."

"Good to hear." Maybe he came to offer him a fulltime job. He had mixed feelings about that. Working fulltime felt like giving up on the writing career. The money and position, however, might impress Natalie.

"I was glad to see you at the party," he said.

Why do I feel a "but" coming? "It's sheer genius to have a Christmas party in January." And by genius, he meant lunacy, but saying so would also be madness.

"How's the novel coming along?" Cunningham asked.

So that was his angle. He worried about him bailing mid-semester. *I'd never do that.* He snapped the cap on the marker, sensing this was no social call. The president didn't just pop in to say hello. Cunningham paced with his hands in his pockets. His words were friendly enough, but his face and tone betrayed him.

"On schedule," Russ confirmed. "I hope to send a final draft to my agent by week's end. But you don't have to worry about me shirking my responsibility to the college. I'm loving the class. Loving the kids. Loving the area. I could definitely see myself putting down roots in Peninsula." *With Natalie.*

Clearing his throat, Cunningham said, "I noticed you brought Mrs. Duncan to the party."

"Natalie?"

"Yes. Natalie Duncan. Mother of Tiffany Duncan, one of your students. Do you think with your history that's wise?"

"My history?" His stomach churned, stirring the acids, heating up his chest. "I was completely up front with you about the reason I left my last position. There was no rule in place at the time barring me from dating another teacher." *Vanessa back to haunt me.*

"But there is now," Dr. Cunningham pointed out. "A rule that was implemented because of you."

He'd like to think Vanessa was the reason the rule was implemented. She was mental. A real piece of work. Yes, it had ended ugly. Russ put his hands on his hips and let out a breath he suddenly realized he'd been holding too long in his lungs. Looking at the ground, he shook his head. *I can't believe this is happening.* Why did he always fall for women who were taboo?

He could see the potential for trouble, for talk and speculation. But this was his personal life they were discussing. He was entitled to a life outside class. Russ was sensible enough to keep his professional life and personal life separate. For the most part.

"Mrs. Duncan is a formidable woman." He cleared his throat. "Take my word for it. Have you ever heard of a woman scorned?"

Not only had a he heard of a woman scorned, he'd seen if first hand. And by all accounts, Russ had been the one scorned. It was just bad form to cheat on a guy, and then be angry when he doesn't forgive you and welcome you back with open arms. The stalking that followed was just overkill. Closely followed by crazy.

"Listen, Dr. Cunningham, with all due respect, I met Natalie before I started work here. I had no idea her daughter would be in my class until we were already involved." His fist clenched around the marker. "It's not going to be an issue."

"Until you give her child a B when she thinks she deserves an A."

"Miss Duncan always does A work," he said flatly. The conversation had gone from concerning to irritating.

"What if the student next to her thinks they do A work?" he asked. "What if they think Tiffany's *not* doing A work?"

"I welcome an audit of my class, as well as the grades I'm assigning." He struggled to keep his voice level, even though his mood was hostile. He was, if nothing else, fair in his grading. "The grades I give are well documented."

"I don't want it to come to an audit," Cunningham said.

"If I have to choose between this job and Natalie, I choose Natalie." Hopefully she felt the same. If their relationship was a poker hand, he was all in. She hadn't folded yet, but she didn't see a winning hand like he did. "That's where I stand."

The door to the classroom swung open. Felicity wandered in early as usual, interrupting the exchange. Russ glanced to the clock on the wall, although he could nearly set a watch by Felicity and her overzealous punctuality.

Turning to her, he asked, "Could you give us a couple minutes, Felicity?"

She turned a little pink, as she was prone to do. "Oh, sure."

Dr. Cunningham held up his hand. "Not necessary. I think we're done. Let's just both do some soul searching about the issue at hand."

"I don't need to," he said. "I've made my position

clear. There is no issue."

Walking backwards toward the door, Dr. Cunningham said, "I hope you're right, Mr. Crew."

Once he exited, Felicity asked, "What was that about?"

He really wanted to vent, tell someone his troubles. Natalie would no doubt cut him loose in an effort to save his career if he told her. She'd grab any excuse to end their relationship. He couldn't tell her. He had no one to unload on.

He combed his fingers through his hair. "Nothing."

Chapter Eleven

"Mrs. Duncan." Russ pulled Natalie into a firm hug. "Damn, don't you look good?"

She felt an adolescent blush heat her face. The way he looked at her made her stomach do somersaults. The way he touched her nearly made *her* actually do somersaults. They'd stolen a few moments during the week for a movie one evening and lunch another day. Friday night was upon them now. Tiffany had overnight plans. It was Lana's weekend to mind the store. They could stay up late and sleep in even later. Together.

She grabbed him by the shirtfront and yanked him through the door of her upstairs loft. "Get in here before the neighbors feel the heat rising off us and call the fire department."

He tripped in as she pulled him into an embrace. Pushing her against a wall, he covered her lips with his. He groaned into her mouth. He investigated her body, for what, she didn't know. The way he kept searching, he hadn't found it yet.

"Where should we do this?" he asked.

"No romance?" She laughed when he found a ticklish spot near her waist. "No sweet talk?"

"I've been thinking about you all week," he breathed his raspy words in her ear. "You're so beautiful." Russ plunged his tongue in her mouth, still searching. From the inside this time. "I'm crazy about you, Nat."

Satisfied with his romantic sweet talk, she angled him toward the bedroom. He pushed. She pulled. They fell across the mattress, rolling back and forth. Clothes peeled away. She'd worn her best lingerie in anticipation of him skimming them slowly down her limbs, leaving kisses where there once had been lace. It went down more like a frenzy, but she enjoyed the passion that seemed uncontainable. They were nearly combustible in their ecstasy, a slow burn of passion suddenly flaming out of control.

On his knees at the foot of her bed, Russ grabbed her hips and dragged her to the edge. She squealed with delight. He randomly peppered her inner thighs with kisses.

"Oh my God," she muttered. She had decided to tell him all about Duane—how he died—how they lived and loved, but it could wait until later or tomorrow. They had time.

He swept his tongue over her center and she dug her heels into the edge of the bed. Her insides heated up, a swirling whirlpool of desire stirred inside her belly.

Standing, Russ braced his thighs against the box spring and mattress. He planted his palms flat on top of the mattress on either side of her head. Natalie draped her legs over his shoulders.

"God, you're beautiful," he said.

His face heated up from his words, his actions, the intense look in his eyes.

When he eased into her, she sighed from the utter completion. He was the cork to her bottle, the key to her lock, the missing piece to her puzzle. The piece you find under the couch after a long, exhaustive search. He showed her the true meaning of fulfillment, which didn't end with a sigh. More like a cry for mercy.

He collapsed into her seconds later, releasing her legs and groaning.

Laid out naked crosswise on the bed, Russ and Natalie clung to one another, breathing heavy, hearts serenading each other with a steady beat. She touched her hand to her chest, feeling the thump of her heart against her fingers. She pressed her palm against his chest to gauge his drumming heartbeat in sync with hers. The pillows lay haphazardly on the floor, quilts and blankets bunched and rumpled at the foot of the bed. All in all they'd created a mess. A beautiful mess.

Natalie traced lazy paths across his damp skin with her fingers. She caressed the red, raised scar on his hip with one hand. Her other hand skimmed his lower lips. Russ gobbled up her finger, making her laugh. With her mouth, she sprinkled kisses along his torso, the last one she planted on his scar.

"It'll fade in time," he said softly, as if promising she wouldn't be saddled with his ugly scar forever.

She nestled into his body. "Want to talk about it?"

He was silent for a beat, and then he cleared his throat. "I was riding my bike to school, as I often did— weather permitting. I'd been training for a triathlon."

Of course you were.

"A car plowed into me." He shrugged. "Bad luck."

There was more to his tale. Natalie didn't know how to drag the information from him, or even if she wanted to. "And."

He tapped his heart with his fist. "My injury is in here."

"Vanessa?"

He nodded. "While I was laid up, she came around less and less." He sniffed, more as a nervous quirk than a prelude to tears, she guessed. "I knew something was up. Wasn't until I was back on my feet I found out the substitute who took over my classes, took over my girlfriend as well. I let him keep her, but I wanted my class back."

She choked out a laugh, sensing he wanted to keep the mood light. "Good on you."

Turning his head, he said, "Vanessa wanted me back."

Who could blame her?

"I'd dove into my writing while rehabilitating. She liked having a writer boyfriend. On paper, I guess I looked better than the substitute teacher. Poor guy. She got a little freaky after that." Russ turned back to Natalie, sweeping her hair off her face.

"Freaky?"

"Stalkerish. Calling me. Calling my family. Following me. " He blew out a breath. "When I didn't reciprocate, she began sabotaging my career with lies. Tainting my reputation. When I got my writing grant, I decided to move on, and away. Working in the same building, much less the same hemisphere was awkward, to say the least."

With her head on his chest, she asked, "What made you come here?"

"Why not here?" Russ cleared his throat again. She could tell emotion bubbled up in him, but he tried to be cool as if he was over the pain. "I took the first job offered, anywhere. It just so happened to be here. Fate, I guess."

She squeezed him tight. "I won't hurt you, Russ."

Absently he combed through her hair with his fingers. "I know, sweetheart."

Looking up into his face, she said, "Do you? Do you really?"

"Of course." Hurt shone in his eyes. "I trust you, Nat. I know you're not her."

She pushed up to kneeling. "Damn right I'm not *her*. Could *she* make lasagna?" It was all prepared in the refrigerator, just waiting to be baked to perfection. She wanted to tell him about Duane, but now wasn't the time, not after he'd bared his soul. It might play out like one-ups-manship.

His lip curled up on one side to a crooked grin. "I never saw any evidence that she could."

Pulling away, she said, "Well, you're about to see evidence that I can."

****

Wearing nothing but an apron and his boxer shorts, Russ centered himself in front of the stove. He flipped the popping bacon with a fork.

Last time he saw Natalie, she was snoozing in her bed. She snored a little, but he didn't mind. Her snore sounded feminine. They'd made love two more times— once after dinner up in the sunroom where they were supposed to be sipping wine while star gazing. And again in the early morning hours before the sun made an appearance in the sky. He loved sleeping with her all night, waking in the dark to find her warmth comforted him after too long alone. He'd never lived with Vanessa. Never really thought about it. He felt compelled to live with Natalie, to fall asleep with her in his arms and wake hearing her soft mutterings.

He'd thought Vanessa was "the one", but now with Natalie, he could see, hear, and feel the difference. It was palpable. He wondered when would be an appropriate waiting period to live together, to tell her he loved her, to ask her to marry him. He wanted—no—needed those things in his life. Her. All day every day.

He nearly jumped out of his skin when a blood-curdling scream rang out behind him.

Turning, he exclaimed, "Tiffany!" Putting his hands out in front of him, he said, "I can explain."

With her hand at her throat, she gasped for air. "You scared the crap out of me."

"This is not what it looks like," he protested. Why? He wasn't sure. It was almost certainly what it looked like, but Natalie would appreciate his denial.

Tiffany scoffed. "Looks like you and my mom have taken *it* to the next level."

Russ plunged his fingers through his hair. *Okay...yeah...so...maybe it is what it looks like.* Natalie wouldn't care for the inferred relationship, but they couldn't fool her daughter forever. "It's not like that."

He heard Natalie's feet slapping on the wood floor. "I can explain."

"Mr. Crew has already sort of explained." Tiffany frowned at his choice of smiley face underwear before turning her disapproval to Natalie draped in nothing but a short, thin robe, hair tousled from sex and sleep.

"It's not what it looks like," Natalie said.

"I already tried that," Russ mumbled.

Mother turned the tables on her daughter. "What are you doing home, young lady?"

Crossing her arms over her chest, Tiffany offered her excuse. "I had a fight with Crystal and Amber."

"My house was being fumigated," Russ explained. "Bugs. Big bugs. Your mother was gracious enough to allow me to stay here. I'm returning the favor by making breakfast. I hope you like eggs, bacon, and hash browns." He braced himself for her to swallow his lie, or not.

Turning and glancing at the couch for a split second, she then eyed him skeptically. "Really?"

"Oh, mind your own beeswax," Natalie said to Tiffany. "We're...together...me and Russ...we're an item...for a while now."

"Since when?" Tiffany demanded.

"We're in love," Russ added. "I love your mom, Tiffany." Turning to Natalie, he said, "I love you, Nat." That answered his question about how long he should wait to tell her he loved her. He should have said it last night or this morning in the heat of passion, but this was better. He loved her in and out of the heat. In and out of bed.

She slapped her hand to her lips. "Oh." She crossed the room to burrow into his embrace. "I love you, too."

They sealed their pledge with a kiss.

"Oh, gross!" Tiffany cried out. "I think I'm going to be sick. Mom. Your robe is open." She spun around and stalked away to her room. "Thank God I'm almost out of here." Her bedroom door slammed.

Russ turned the burner down. "On the subject of Tiffany being out of here, let's live together. Not now. Not today. In the fall. When she goes to college. What do you say?"

"I say yeah."

"Life is good," he said.

"Life *is* good," she agreed.

****

Things remained awkward between Natalie and Tiffany days later. She denied having any objection to her mother dating her teacher. She wouldn't have a leg to stand on in a court of law since she'd thrown them together. Too bad this wasn't one of those court of law situations. Natalie guessed the hurt came from the betrayal. Russ had been right. They should have told her up front about the relationship. He was so much more mature than her.

She decided to abdicate to him on all matters of morality and honesty in the future.

Tiffany shuffled to the breakfast table wearing a ratty robe and fuzzy slippers. She yawned. Natalie, already up and dressed, set a mug of tea on the kitchen table for her daughter as an offering of peace.

"Thanks." Tiff plopped in a chair at the table, wrapping her hands around the cup.

"Tired?" Natalie inquired. She'd heard her come in late from her study group, which was probably more of a party or a date. She had to trust Tiffany to be responsible, just like Russ suggested on numerous occasions, difficult as that was.

"Yeah." Tiffany rubbed her eyes. "What a day? Didn't sleep well. You?"

"I slept fine." Or she slept fine after she heard Tiff come in. Six to eight hours of rest and she was good to go. "You're not still upset about me dating Russ, are you?" Natalie prepared herself to point out that Tiffany had set them up, even though they'd already been together off and on before the set up.

"No, Mom." Tiffany shook her head. "I'm a little ruffled by how it all went down. I don't think I know the whole story."

Natalie doubted she knew everything Tiffany was up to either. She knew for a fact that as a teenager, her parents had no idea about her sneaking out at night, meeting up with Duane or about their backseat escapades. Not until the damage was done, anyhow.

"I just want you to be happy when I leave for college," Tiffany said. "I'm worried about you being alone, filling the lonely void with a collection of cats. I know you have Aunt Lana and Uncle Clint and the store, but I want you to have a life. Is that too much to ask?"

She slid into a chair across from Tiffany. "That's why you set me and Russ up?"

"Yeah. He's cool." She shrugged. "Sort of. I didn't expect to come home and find him cooking nearly in the buff though."

Pursing her lips, Natalie asked, "You don't think he's a little too young for me?"

"He's old." Tiffany rolled her eyes. "You're old. What difference does it make how old? Old is old."

Old was not old, any more than young was young. Between the ages of sixteen and eighteen, the age of Tiff's new boyfriend, lay too many inappropriate years. Natalie still worried about the inappropriateness that rested between twenty-six and thirty-five, or thirty-six and forty-five. And so on. *How will I look at sixty-five to his fifty-six?*

"Aren't you going to be late for class?" she asked.

Tiffany was commonly so punctual and with near perfect attendance. Natalie worried again or still that her daughter did not possess the maturity for this foray into collegiate life. Emotionally she was a high schooler, not equipped for the distractions of parties and boys without proper supervision. Natalie had been trying to give her more freedom to make her own decisions and choices. And here she sat, tired, cranky, possibly hung over, and about to be late for class.

Tiffany tilted her head. "Class is cancelled. Didn't Mr. Crew—Russ tell you?"

"No." She'd called him, leaving a message, but he hadn't returned her call. She figured he'd been grading papers or writing, needing some peace and quiet. She tried to respect the solitude he required. "Why? What happened?" News of his class being cancelled alarmed her. "Is Russ okay?"

"Felicity." Tiffany rolled her eyes. "She made an allegation that Russ—Mr. Crew had an inappropriate relationship with her. No one believes it, Mom. And you shouldn't either. The girl has been needy and clingy since day one."

"What?" *Why wouldn't he tell me?* "Since when?"

Tiffany shrugged. "I've heard rumors this isn't the first time she's pulled this crap."

"Language," Natalie warned her absently.

"There's a hearing or inquiry or something today at nine." Tiffany shrugged. "I'm sure he'll be cleared of any wrong doing. He's totally into you, Mom. He shied away from Felicity like she was a week old fish stinking up the classroom."

"I've got to go. Be there." First she picked up the phone to call Russ. His phone rang and rang, finally going to voice mail. She left a message. Looking at the clock on the wall, she had to go if she wanted to be there in time. She barely had time to stop by his apartment first. "Will you be all right?"

"Go, Mom."

****

Russ' head pounded like a drum, even in sleep. His temples throbbed. He swallowed a couple times to be rid of the cottonmouth plaguing his slumber. His eyes squinted open when he heard his name being called outside of his dream.

"Russ!" Pound, pound, pound. "Open the door."

A muffled voice from next door said, "Shut up, lady!"

Russ couldn't agree more. One eye attempted to focus on the clock next to his bed. *Too early for so much racket.* He swallowed a couple times trying to scare up some saliva to no avail.

"Russ!"

His eyes flew open, shooting a piercing pain to the center of his forehead. "Natalie," he grumbled under his breath. Calling her had been on his to-do list before he'd gotten trashed. *Note to self—make important calls before cracking open the bottle.*

Rolling out of bed, he landed to the floor on all fours. Using the bed as leverage, he pushed up to standing. He did a zombie walk to the front door, arms outstretched on account of his blurry vision. He stumbled over his shoes and fumbled with the lock and the doorknob.

"Hey, Nat," he said. She looked out of focus. A blurry blob in his hallway. But there was no mistaking her voice.

"Don't *hey, Nat* me," she said.

With his finger to his lips, he shushed her. "Not so loud."

She pushed past him. "Are you hung over?"

"I might still be drunk." He headed in the direction of the kitchenette. Turning on the kitchen faucet, he leaned in and guzzled water from the spigot. He wasn't sure what Natalie was doing. His sense of depth perception was distorted, along with his equilibrium. "Ow!" he hollered when she nailed him in the back of the head with a shirt, boxer shorts, and a pair of socks that all fell to the floor at his feet, despite his attempt to catch at least one article of clothing.

"Get dressed," she said. He could clearly see now she was digging through his dresser, probably for clean jeans. "We don't have time for a shower."

"Who said anything about a shower?" He sniffed his armpits and decided a shower would be in his best interest. He peeled his T-shirt over his head, dropping the soiled one to the floor next to the others.

Natalie snatched the clean shirt from the floor where it fell and yanked it on over his head. "According to Tiff, your hearing is in twenty minutes."

Now I remember. "Yeah, I'm not going." He poked his arms through the sleeves. Not because he wanted to be dressed, it seemed the path of least resistance.

"Did you do something wrong?" she asked. "Did you have a relationship with that girl?" Her tone was not to be taken seriously. He'd mock her or challenge her if he had his wits about him.

"I sure did." He teetered on unsteady legs. "A teacher-student relationship. I taught her everything I know about Hemmingway." *And this is the thanks I get.* He'd seen the look of adoration in the eyes of plenty of students in the past. Nothing like this had ever happened although he guessed it was just a matter of time. "You always knew I'd fall for a younger woman, didn't you?" He laughed.

"You *are* still drunk."

"Yes, ma'am."

"Go brush your teeth, Russ." Her tone was that of a parent at the end of rational reason. "You reek of alcohol."

"You can't fix this, Nat." He staggered to the bathroom to do as ordered.

Sure, part of him needed to fight for his tarnished honor. The drunk part of him wanted to call it a day and go back to bed. The drunk in him won. He locked himself in the bathroom where he climbed into the shower with his clothes on. He took advantage of the rush of water to drown out the sound of her protests on the other side of the door.

Eventually she gave up and left. Her voice continued to echo around in his conscience long after her departure.

****

Natalie opened the door to the conference room and stood against the back wall. There weren't too many people in attendance. She guessed this was the equivalent of an arraignment or preliminary hearing or whatever. They wanted to evaluate the merits of Felicity's allegations. Natalie did, too.

The girl sat primly with her hands folded on her lap. She couldn't look sweeter or more innocent if she donned a nun's habit.

"This is a closed door meeting," Dr. Cunningham said to Natalie without actually looking at her, as if she were an annoyance. Okay, yes, she had perhaps been annoying to him in the past, challenging the idea of Tiffany taking college classes. And there was a good chance she'd be an irritant today.

"I'm here on behalf of Russ Crew," she protested. "I might be able to shed some light on the matter." *Probably not.*

"We'd like Mr. Crew to shed some light on the matter." He glanced at the clock on the wall. It was ten after nine. No Russ.

"He's…he's under the weather." To say the least. In his condition he was likely to burst in and quote Tolstoy or Steinbeck. "He asked me to come unless we can postpone for another day." *Pretty, pretty please.*

Cunningham sighed. He waved in Felicity's direction. "Go on, Felicity."

She cleared her throat, disregarding Natalie with a look of derision before continuing with her rendition of her fantastical account of her relationship with Russ. Her words cut like a knife into Natalie's gut, even though she knew the girl lied. She appeared so young and untouched, the picture of innocence tarnished by her instructor. Taken advantage of. Used. The administrators and instructors in attendance were eating it up. If she didn't know Russ better, she might have taken up a torch and pitchfork and labeled him a monster.

Natalie raised her hand. "Excuse me. May I ask a question?" She really wanted to go all crazy-cougar on them, but knew she'd come off looking nuts, thereby adding credence to Felicity's story. No one objected outside the looks of irritation directed at her. "Felicity? Are you saying you began your relationship with Mr. Crew the night of the library get-together?"

She squared her shoulders. "That's right."

Natalie's heartbeat pulsed, thumping loudly in her

ears. "About what time, may I ask?"

Her eyes narrowed, as if trying to figure her inquisitors angle in order to thwart her plan. "Nine-thirty or nine-forty-five."

"Russ dropped Felicity off first," Natalie said. All eyes were on her. "He brought Tiffany home last. She'd attest to that fact."

The eyes swung back to Felicity. She swallowed hard. "He came back after dropping her off. Rather clever of him, don't you think? Making Tiffany his alibi."

"Tiffany invited him up." Natalie made eye contact with several people, hoping they could see the truth in her eyes. "We talked over coffee and chocolate chip cookies." She figured details were a good idea. "Tiffany can verify. He was at our place until well after ten."

"It might have been later," she protested. "When he showed up. Might have been later. I may have dozed off. Lost track of time."

Natalie held up her hands. "Okay. Fair enough. Go on." She didn't want to spook her, just rattle her a bit, knock some holes in her story. Create doubt. These people were educators and administrators. They didn't need a scandal rocking the small school. Hopefully they wanted the truth.

Felicity dove headfirst back into her tale of misconduct and betrayal. She was most convincing. Her rendition was short on details. Dates, times, places. What her story lacked in facts, it made up for in soap-opera-like gossip.

Dr. Cunningham cleared his throat when she finished. "I wish Mr. Crew were here to defend himself."

"May I...may I ask a few questions?" She'd heard it wasn't wise for an attorney to ask a question they didn't know how the witness would answer, but Natalie wanted there to be no doubt. She had faith in Russ and needed these people to share her certainty. "I know you've been through a great deal, Felicity." She approached her. Listening to the girl caused her own animosity to fall away, leaving only pity for her. She must have suffered some sort of trauma. But not at the hands of Russ. "I hate to ask this. You've seen Mr. Crew naked?"

Her cheeks pinked up. "Of course." Felicity's eyes closed slowly over her eyes. "Many times."

"Then you can tell us of a very distinctive...uh...mark on his body?" Natalie said.

Dr. Cunningham's brow drew together. "Like a tattoo or a birthmark?"

Looking straight at the girl, she connected with her through a shared stare. "Felicity will know."

She recognized panic and anger in Felicity's face, which transitioned from pink with embarrassment, to red with rage. "A scar."

Natalie's stomach felt like it dropped to her feet. Anyone could have guessed a scar, she told herself. Russ walked with a slight limp. Felicity was a smart girl. "Yes. Where?"

"Enough," Russ said from the back of the room.

Natalie spun around. She hadn't seen or heard him enter. Dark circles framed his bloodshot eyes, but he looked better than he had earlier when she'd rousted him out of bed.

He raked his fingers through his hair and sighed. "She's been through enough."

Chapter Twelve

Russ couldn't stand to see Natalie defending him to the room of judgmental cynics. He wouldn't stand by and watch Felicity be thrown deeper into whatever mental illness she suffered from. Clearly she was a troubled girl. He neither wanted to contribute further to her suffering nor cause her any additional pain. Yesterday—yes—bring it. Today—no.

"Felicity and I have no relationship outside that of teacher and student." He dragged his hand along his face, his whiskers scrubbing against his palm. "I've never given her any reason to think otherwise. We've never—" Russ couldn't bring himself to say the word. His stomach roiled, bile rising in his throat. "She's never seen me naked, I assure you."

"That's not true!" Felicity objected. "His knee. The scar is on his knee." She pointed at his bum leg.

Good guess, but that's all it was. "I have a rather prominent scar on my hip from an auto accident, not that it's any business of you people. If you're not convinced, provide me with dates and times of alleged acts of...of inappropriate behavior and I'll do my best to refute them." His time had been divided between Natalie, class, and writing. He kept detailed notes about appointments with students and faculty.

Felicity dropped her face to her hands and wept. "He can't love you," she sobbed. "Why would he want *you* when he could have me?"

"I'm sorry, Felicity." After all she'd put him through, he had nothing but pity for her. "It's always been Natalie."

"Why?" she wailed.

Russ didn't have an answer for her except *the heart wants what the heart wants*. His heart ached seeing the pain in Natalie's eyes. He wished his public declaration convinced her that he loved her above any other. From the moment she opened her mouth and asked if he were dangerous. By her weary appearance, all she heard was Felicity's rankled inquiry about why he'd want Nat over her. Neither woman could reconcile his choice. Perhaps Natalie knew something about herself that he didn't. Maybe she knew best. Possibly everyone knew better than him who he should love and why.

"And I quit," he added.

"Russ," Natalie protested, "no."

He couldn't look at her. Knowing without a doubt he did nothing wrong didn't stop him from feeling lousy. Guilty. Maybe it was the hangover talking. He might regret his words and actions tomorrow, but for now he earned them and owned them. With his head bowed, he turned the knob and stepped out, closing the door behind him.

His hollow steps echoed in the empty hallway. He hadn't made it to the stairs before he heard Natalie call after him. His heart lurched. He slowed, but didn't stop.

When she caught up, she grabbed his arm. "Where are you going?"

"Home to sleep *it* off." He stopped, turning to her. *So beautiful. So brave.* "Can we talk later?" He did his best impression of aloofness. Indifference. She didn't make his detachment easy for him. Here, now, he wanted to crush her in an embrace. Thank her for believing in him. Apologize for putting her through this. He wanted to crawl inside her. She was home to him. He had no idea what he was to her.

She said she loved him, but he'd put her on the spot. She'd said they have a future. Not until the fall. Even though that was his proffered compromise. She could have suggested he move in sooner. Breaking his lease was idiotic. He wasn't thinking clearly.

She planted her hands on her hips. "In your dreams."

So bossy. He snickered through his pain. "I'm beat, Nat. If I don't sleep, I'm going to drop."

"You love to teach," she said, her voice laced with empathy and confusion.

"One more love struck student, Nat and I can kiss my teaching career goodbye, guilty or not." His passion was for writing. Teaching was his fallback position, but he did love being an educator. He wanted to do both. For some reason he wasn't able to keep his private life from bleeding over into his professional life. Maybe he was as immature as she believed him to be.

Natalie pointed down the hall toward the hearing room where people filed out. "She obviously lied."

He did not want to put Natalie through this again. He didn't want to go through it again either. The Felicity incident was every bit as stressful as the Vanessa episode, and would probably prove to be just as hard to get over. What was next? A literary groupie stalker? The movie *Misery* played on a loop in his alcohol soaked brain. He'd never again be able to teach without being guarded. More guarded. Too guarded to be an effective educator.

"Can we please not rehash this here or now?" He desperately wanted the incident to disappear. But sex scandals rarely did.

She narrowed her eyes at him. "I do need to get to the shop."

"Go." He waved his hand. "We'll talk later."

Natalie leaned in and kissed his cheek. "I'll see you tonight." Her statement sounded like orders to be obeyed, or else.

"Of course." He faked a smile. "Thanks for the rescue."

****

The sound of the blender grated on Natalie's nerves as much as the blades grated on the ice, slicing and dicing them into manageable pieces.

Lana glided across Natalie's living room with a fruity blended pink drink in each hand. "Doctor's orders."

"Doctor? What doctor?" Natalie scoffed, but she felt on the verge of tears again.

"Dr. Lush." Lana winked. "Won't you and I have a blast in rehab making fun of the other drunks?"

"That's not nice." She laughed in spite of her sadness. Her sister did that to her, making her chuckle on purpose, and sometimes quite by accident. "I don't think they have two-for-one specials at rehab, Lana."

"Pity."

They clinked glasses before sipping the mixed concoction. According to her sister there was nothing that couldn't be fixed with a cocktail, a shopping spree, or a spa day. They'd already partaken in all three and were making a second pass at the cocktails.

Lana stirred her drink with a straw. "What's the latest?"

Natalie sighed. "Haven't heard from him."

Russ had packed his meager belongings and vacated his apartment the same day of the hearing. No forwarding address. Now she knew how he'd felt when she'd ditched him.

"Every lead is a dead end." Not that she had many leads to his whereabouts. Phone number disconnected. Email address changed.

"We should go shoe shopping," Lana said.

"Shoe shopping?" Sure, maybe Russ took a temp job at the mall as a shoe salesman. *It could happen.* He'd realize his folly when he stuffs her size six-and-a-half foot into a size six glass pump, Prince Charming style, and finds out she's not his royal match. "How's that going to help?"

"Shoes make everything better," Lana stated her absurd factoid like God's-honest-truth.

"I shouldn't have pushed him away over and over and over again." She sighed again, for about the thousandth time since he'd left. Left her. You push hard enough for long enough, even the most steadfast objects move. Or was it a case of *what you fear you create*? She threw him away out of fear of losing him and now she'd done just that. Lost him. For good.

"Pish." Lana waved her hand. "He'll be back." She was working on her third girlie drink, but didn't have heartache to keep her sober like Natalie did.

"It's been three weeks," she said. "Without a word."

He'd made a clean break of it with a heartfelt note taking all the blame. He didn't want to hurt her, blah,

blah, blah. He needed to be alone, yada, yada, yada. To think. To write. To forget.

"Do you think he'll pen a novel about you?" Lana asked.

"Of course not." She wondered who'd play her in the movie version. Probably some no-talent-washed-up-over-the-hill-has-been.

"Stalk him online," Lana suggested.

Did I just fall off a turnip truck? She'd spent countless hours searching the internet. As an author, he'd have to come out of the incognito closet sooner or later. "He holds the information super highway and all its impersonality in much disdain."

The oven timer dinged.

Mid-slurp, Lana waved her hand over her head. After swallowing, she said, "Nachos are ready." She grimaced. "Brain-freeze-brain-freeze-brain-freeze."

Natalie shook her head slowly back and forth.

Her emotional meltdown was all the excuse Lana needed to go off the wagon and off her diet. She sashayed away to the kitchen, returning with a mother-load of tortilla chips smothered in melted cheese, taco meat, and onions, topped with jalapenos. On the side was the mother of all sour cream dollops, guacamole and salsa, too. It was a recipe for heartburn to go along with her heartbreak.

"Good gravy, Lana," Natalie said. "It looks like death by cheese." A gooey, greasy orgy of food.

Pulling the plate toward her, Lana said, "So you don't want any?"

"I didn't say that." She leaned in to help herself directly from the serving dish. *Who needs plates, utensils, or napkins?* She'd lost roughly eight pounds she couldn't afford to lose since Russ departed. Her appetite returned when the spicy scent of the nachos reached her nose. At first she thought her broken heart would never mend. Seemed three weeks was all she needed to get on the road to recovery. By this same time next year, Natalie would be good as new. Probably. Or not. Dredging a chip through the salsa, she said, "I don't want to be rude after you went to all the trouble."

Lana rolled her eyes.

****

Three months later, Natalie only thought of Russ a few times a day: namely, morning, noon, and night. Besides that, her life had returned to pre-Russ normal, she thought, as she sat behind her antique roll-top desk at the shop. She went to work, came home, and doted on Tiffany, who rebelled against the doting. Natalie was on the fast track to being alone and lonely by autumn. Sure, she could do a Risky Business dance wearing only her underwear across the hardwood floor of the loft, but the idea simply didn't appeal to her.

Mother and daughter applied for grants, scholarships, and student loans, all the things Natalie never had a chance to do for herself as a young adult. The chore also cured her of ever wanting to do it again. Together they toured a few local campuses. They compromised on which colleges to apply to and readied for Tiffany's high school graduation, a year too early in Natalie's opinion. She wished she had the luxury of the additional year to prepare for an empty nest, although she knew for a while it was coming.

"Did you order anything?" Lana asked, gazing out the front window to the street.

"Don't think so," Natalie replied absently. "Why?"

"UPS is here." Lana loved the UPS man, ogling him unmercifully like a slab of prime meat. Poor man probably dreaded making a delivery. Or loved it. Who knew?

She stepped outside to sign for the package. Natalie shook her head, listening to her sister laugh and carry on. Lucky the driver didn't take her flirting seriously. Lana would probably lay him out cold or complain to his superior if he reciprocated. She mostly flirted with men she wouldn't ever date. The men she dated and subsequently married, all had oodles of money. She was between husbands at the moment.

The bell chimed when Natalie's sister returned. She assessed the packages critically. "One for Tiff and one for you."

Without looking up from her computer screen, she said, "From?"

"Russ Crew." Lana's eyebrows nearly hit her hairline.

Natalie's jaw dropped to her chest. "What? Why now? I was nearly over him."

Lana snorted a laugh. "You want I should throw them in the trash?" She played her own version of keep-away, holding the packages out of reach, and yet strategically hovering over the trash can.

"Give 'em."

Lana handed the first package addressed to her. She tore into the contents. "His manuscript." Her fingers caressed his name typed in black across the smooth paper. In red ink he wrote, *as promised*, followed by his signature in a scrolling cursive and the date. "How cruel."

"Cruel?"

"Yes, cruel." She picked up the loose leafed bundle of papers, bringing the pages to her nose, sniffing them. No scent of Russ lingered on the pages, but he must have touched them at some point. "To taunt me just when I was about to accept a dinner invite from Tony down at the metal works."

Lana sneered at her. "No you weren't."

She'd known Tony for years. He did the occasional welding repair for her. Some sandblasting too. Nice enough guy. He'd been working up the nerve for a while. It was uncomfortable to be around him, stammering and staring at his shoes unable to look her in the eyes. "Was, too. You don't know."

"Open this one." Lana handed over the second package.

Heavy. "It's addressed to Tiffany." Clearly a book of some kind rested inside. Unlike her gift from Russ, Natalie felt the hardcover of a book. "A graduation present." *Sweet of him to think of her. Of us both.* She'd half expected him to surprise her and show up for Tiffany's graduation. No such luck. The packages told her he'd be a no show.

"No phone number?" Lana inquired.

Natalie shook her head.

"Address?"

General delivery. Palisades, Washington. "Oh, my God."

Lana twisted, trying to read the address. "What?"

"I know where he is." Or was, as of two days ago.

****

Russ sat casually slumped in an uncomfortable chair at the only coffee shop in town. Also the only place in town besides the small library that had wifi. Slow, spotty wifi that left much to be desired. But the coffee at the shop was pretty good—strong, the way he liked it. And the library proved to be a quiet place to work.

He gulped the last drink from his cup.

Scrolling through his email, a blur of familiar green caught his eye out the window. *Nothing.* Just his mind playing tricks. Again. He often saw Natalie or her car where it wasn't. He'd hear her laughter on the wind. He dreamed of her at night. Too many songs on the radio reminded him of her, of them together and apart. Movies. Books. Commercials. Everything forced him to pine for her.

He fished his prepaid mobile phone out of his pocket. Scrolling to the desired number, he pressed a single button. His thumb had hovered over the number many times over the past few months. He'd even drunk dialed her a couple times, hanging up after listening to her recorded voice. His drug of choice. He'd stare at the Junque Décor website for hours, imagining her snapping the photos or writing the blurbs and updates on the site.

The phone rang in his ear. His heart raced. Her voicemail kicked on, followed by a beep. "Hey, Nat. Natalie. It's...it's Russ." *Smooth.* "I wanted to talk to you." *Obviously.* "I'll phone you back...later...another time." *Way to state the obvious, Russ.* "Just...you know...wanted to make sure you got my package." He disconnected. He knew she got the packages unless Lana tossed them in a dumpster.

He twisted the ring on his pinky. He should return the band of gold, but it reminded him of her. The ring gave him confidence when he felt none. It gave him a reason to someday pop in on her, if only for the excuse of returning the ring.

He wasn't sure what he thought had changed in the last few months. She was probably still self-conscious of the age difference between them. That was unfixable. Russ continued to feel the burn of Felicity's treachery. Vanessa's too. He must be a masochist to want to enlist for a third round of pain at the hands of another woman. Natalie wasn't just another woman.

She's not like that.

She'd probably moved on by now. He had to know for sure if they were finished. He had no one to blame but himself for the breakup she hadn't requested, and he'd never wanted.

****

Natalie bounced down the dirt road, her shocks tested by the ruts and rocks. The topography looked nothing like it had a few short months earlier covered in snow. Hues of brown and green replaced the stark white. A curl of smoke rose from the chimney of the lodge that appeared a whole lot more welcoming in the spring than it had in the dead of winter.

The cabins flanking the winding river looked less shabby in the full sun with a carpet of green around them. Maybe they'd been treated to a fresh coat of paint. She didn't see Russ' pickup truck in sight though. She parked, and then tramped to the office door, peeking through the window she had vandalized in the past.

Pushing through the door, she smiled brightly and said, "Hello." Natalie hadn't anticipated feeling so rotten about her previous stay at the cabins. Best not to mention breaking in and making herself at home.

"May I help you?" the woman behind the counter asked. She was dressed casually in a plaid over-shirt and jeans.

"I hope so." *Try not to look like a stalker.* "I'm looking for a Russ Crew. Is he staying here?"

"Checked out this morning," she replied.

No. No. No. "Did he say where he was headed?" she asked nonchalantly as if the information meant very little to her, instead of how it actually felt—life and death serious.

"He didn't." She appeared to know more than she was letting on, either that or Natalie was paranoid. "I'm sorry. Are you the one?"

"The one?"

She tilted her head. "The one who broke his heart."

She clutched at her throat. "He told you that?" Russ didn't share his feelings with just anyone.

"Didn't have to."

Sighing, Natalie said, "Yes. Yes, I guess maybe I am, in a roundabout sort of way. But to be fair, he broke mine, too."

"He enjoys the coffee shop in Palisades, as well as the library. But I got the impression he was moving on."

God, I hope not. If she couldn't move on, he shouldn't be able to either. It only reinforced the truth that she loved him more than he loved her. And she could live with that. "Thank you." She turned and exited, wondering if Russ had shared with her his amusing tale of being snowed in here.

Her shoulders sagged. The weight of her feet nearly quadrupled, or so it seemed. Her hand rested on the handle of the car door. She abandoned the handle, heading for the rush of fast moving water in the distance. Due to the spring thaw, the water tested the banks of the stream she remembered from Christmastime. Lazily she meandered down river.

Reaching out for him, he wasn't there. *Where are you, Russ?*

Would he even be happy to see her? His package was nothing more than a promise fulfilled. He'd made no declaration of love or of missing her. She had a fantasy of rapping her knuckles on the cabin door and him scooping her up in an embrace, never letting her go again.

Rubbish.

Natalie's phone beeped, suddenly getting a signal in the remote location. Her heart nearly skipped a beat until she noted the *private* number. *Probably a telemarketer. Again.* They'd left a message about thirty minutes earlier. But after a couple more steps she lost the signal and was unable to get it back.

She sighed, and headed for her car.

****

"She's where?" Russ waved his hands wildly.

He'd returned to Peninsula nearly on autopilot. He had to know where he and Natalie stood—together or apart. He probably stood stooped over in the doghouse for leaving her the way he had. She stood like the conquering hero with the heel of her boot on his neck. And rightly so. He'd be apologizing for a very long time. He'd spend the rest of his life making it up to her. If she'd have him.

He'd thrown in the towel after he'd admonished her so many times for trying to do the same. He'd asked her to have faith in him, and then he failed to have faith in her. She was rubbing off on him, but saying so would only make it look like he blamed her. *Wonder if I could get away with blaming her. Nah.*

"She went to Palisades, Russ." Lana had her cell phone out, attempting to phone Natalie. "To find you." Holding the phone to her ear, she added, "What did you think she'd do once she noticed where the package came from?"

Throwing up his hands in anguish again, he said, "Well?"

"It's going to voicejail." Lana rolled her eyes.

"Service is spotty up there." Everything was spotty. Cell coverage. Internet. Cable TV. It had been a quiet month. Before that he'd bummed around the Washington and Oregon coasts, his truck being his home when he couldn't find a cheap motel.

Lana proceeded to leave a message for Natalie.

Home base for Russ had become cabin number one. He wasn't sure what made him return to the scene of the crime. Where she'd stolen his heart. The cabin in the woods brought him emotionally closer to her, even though he was far away, geographically speaking.

"I'm going back," he said.

"No." Lana fisted the fabric of his shirt. "Don't. This has all the makings of a disaster where one or both of you ends up dead while pursuing the other. Romeo and Juliet you are not."

He dragged his hand along the length of his face. "I can't just sit here waiting."

Lana's cell phone jingled. Russ' heart lurched. Maybe it was Natalie returning her sister's call. He nearly hyperventilated at the thought of speaking to her.

"Oh, no," Lana droned into the phone, her eyes slowly shutting. "Not again."

"What?" Russ made a move for the phone. "Is that Natalie?"

Shaking her head, she mouthed, "Clint." Resting her fingers over the mouthpiece, she said, "Mud slide. Road is washed out just this side of Palisades." She nodded, acknowledging Clint, repeating his words. "Heavy snow last winter. Unusually warm weather this spring. Mudslides. Not at all uncommon. But…"

"But what?"

"Deadly." Her face drained of color. "There are unconfirmed fatalities. It's like last winter all over again."

She turned away to share some private words with her brother. Russ made good use of the time by worrying and pacing. Hanging up, she returned her attention to him.

"Clint's on his way from work," she said, doing her best impression of someone with her emotions in check. The concern leaked through around her eyes. "He'll get ready and head out."

"It'll be getting dark by then," Russ said. "I'm ready to go now." Sitting around waiting for a call was not an option. He needed a task.

He stuffed a list of phone numbers and instructions to call them in order of importance—Lana being call one—once he located Natalie.

Lana grabbed his arm. "You know Duane was struck by lightning, right?"

"Seriously?" he said. "No, I didn't."

"Forces of nature have been out to get *her* since before she was born," Lana said. "Do not die. She'd never recover."

"Got it." He turned to leave, but it wasn't his safety he worried about.

She yanked him back. "And don't let her die."

"Goes without saying."

****

Natalie pulled into the rest stop shortly after dusk. No coffee or cookies this time. All she needed was the restroom, and then she'd be back on the road. Her trip had been a bust, but she couldn't have avoided the jaunt. She could hardly regret it even now. Her only regret would have been if she hadn't taken a chance. Ambling along the banks of the creek had been a nice stroll down Memory Lane. She'd hoped for some closure, but no. The gash in her heart remained wide open.

Assessing her reflection in the bathroom mirror, she decided she looked tired. Old. Good thing she hadn't found Russ. Her next plan—wait until his book was published and show up at a book signing looking fantastic. She'd gone six years without sex. She could go another six. Probably. Hopefully he'd make the writing career happen before that. Reading his novel last night cover to cover, she knew he'd be published soon, if there was any justice in the literary world.

Natalie stopped for a sip of water from the fountain outside the restrooms. Her eyes focused on a man loitering near the car, peeking in the windows. *Don't let him be dangerous. Or a nuisance.* She had nothing to use as a weapon. *Don't make eye contact. Too late.*

He headed toward her with fast paced determination. *Russ!* She froze in place, a breath trapped in her throat.

He broke into a jog. "Nat! Thank God." He enveloped her in a warm, strong embrace like she feared she'd never feel again. "We were so worried."

We? "What? Worried?" Her mind hadn't caught up to the hug, his words or the fact he was at a rest stop. The same rest stop she was at. *What are the odds?* Damn him, he looked amazing.

"Don't you check your cell phone messages?" he asked.

"It's dead." She pinched herself. Maybe this was a dream. *Ow. No. Not a dream.*

"Haven't you been listening to the news?" He held her at arm's length, shaking her lightly.

"No." The world looked out of focus, fuzzy around the edges. His questions made very little sense. "Bon Jovi." She pointed to her car where Bon Jovi had a permanent home in her CD changer.

"There was a mud slide outside of Palisades." He drew her back into a solid hug. "We feared the worst."

There was that word again. *We.* "We who?"

"Lana, Clint, and Tiffany."

"Why is it that natural disasters follow me?" *Who cares?* She burrowed into his chest, absorbing his warmth, reveling in the familiar scent of his skin.

Russ swayed her in his arms "Better they follow than precede you."

Natalie had questions. At the moment all she cared about was a little affection therapy in his arms. "I've missed you," she said.

"I love you."

"Me, too."

He held her at arm's length. "Thank you, Natalie, for rescuing me."

She squinted. "During the blizzard? I think it's safe to say we rescued each other."

He pulled her closed for another hug. "No, not during the blizzard."

Epilogue

Natalie pulled to the curb in front of the multi-story dormitory behind her station wagon.

A lot had happened over the past few months. She'd bought a new car. One befitting a woman with no child to chauffer around, but roomy enough to go junking. An SUV. Tiffany took possession of the station wagon. It was dependable and got good gas mileage for the drive to and from Oregon where she'd decided to go to college. It wasn't Natalie's first choice—too far. It wasn't Tiffany's first choice either, which had been way too far. Oregon was a compromise.

Tiffany popped out of the driver's side of the station wagon, all smiles and nervous energy. Natalie could see and feel her excitement despite the distance of a car length between them. Russ climbed out of the passenger seat of the station wagon. He waved and smiled, and then screwed up his face to make her laugh, which she did. Natalie had driven with her for the first half of the journey. Russ took the second shift. Natalie appreciated the time alone to reflect on the next part of her life. Her life with Russ.

She wanted to drink in the moment. She'd dreaded this day for so long. Now that the day was upon her, she felt rather calm—almost Zen about it. Russ could have all the credit for her serenity since he'd talked her off so many emotional ledges over the past couple months. He knew her so well and loved her anyhow.

"Mom," Tiffany called.

Natalie snapped out of her trance and nodded. Russ had the hatchback open, filling his arms with Tiffany's possessions. Natalie had to give him credit. He didn't act in any hurry to have Tiffany gone. He really enjoyed her. A blessing. She had the ability to test the patience of even those nearest and dearest to her. Same as her mother.

Russ waved Natalie over to help. She'd much rather sit and watch than lend a hand in tossing her daughter out of the nest. How did mother birds manage? Mustering the strength from somewhere, she opened her car door and joined them.

"How you holding up?" Russ asked.

She faked a smile. "Better than expected."

He winked at her. "That's my girl."

After a few trips back and forth between the cars and the dorm, Tiffany's clothes and essentials were in her room. They'd stopped for lunch along the way. Natalie was running out of excuses to stay.

"We should get going." Russ slung an arm around Tiffany and giving her shoulder a squeeze.

"So soon?" Natalie said. "I thought we'd help her decorate." The bed should be made, her boxes needed to be unpacked and curtains would give her some privacy as well as brightening the drab room.

"Why?" He chuckled. "She'll just rearrange everything after we leave. Am I right?" He jostled Tiffany like a rag doll, making her laugh.

"Right," she said. "Besides, I just got a text. Ronnie is waiting for me at the campus coffee shop."

She beamed a radiant smile. "We have orientation later."

Natalie knew how her daughter felt. Men had a way of warming every damp, dark corner of a woman's heart. And after meeting Ronnie, Natalie couldn't find many reasons to dislike him. She'd tried. She was actually relieved Tiffany had someone to depend on in case of an emergency. She could do worse.

"Tell him we said hi." Russ kissed Tiffany's temple and released her.

She rolled her eyes. "I will."

Natalie opened her arms wide. "Give me a hug and then we'll go. Promise." They hugged and squeezed and clung. But neither cried. Maybe in the car on the way home she'd open the floodgates. "We'll see you at Thanksgiving, if not sooner."

"Okay," Tiffany said.

Russ held his thumb and pinky to his ear. "Call us. Often. Or else." He pointed his *or else* finger at her.

"All right, all right."

One more hug and they slowly made their way to the car. She surveyed the busy campus and all the college kids going here or there. She thought she'd be full of regrets for missing out on college life, but no. She liked where she was and who she was and wouldn't change a thing.

Russ folded his hand into hers. "You want me to drive?"

"No. I'm good."

"Are you sure?" He took the car keys from her hand. "I'm waiting for the mental meltdown. Better to do that sort of thing in the passenger seat, if you know what I mean."

"I think I'm going to be okay."

He pointed to the horizon. "Did you see those storm clouds moving in?"

Natalie looked toward the direction of the clouds in question. She sighed. "I don't care what Mother Nature throws at me. I can handle it."

"I know you can, but I wish she'd stop testing you," Russ said.

She snatched the keys from his grasp. "You and me both."

A word about the author...

Kelly Fitzpatrick lives by the sea. Her passion by day is writing. In the evenings she walks barefoot along the sandy beach, the salty water lapping at her feet.
http://www.kellyfitzbooks.blogspot.com

Thank you for purchasing
this publication of The Wild Rose Press, Inc.

If you enjoyed the story, we would appreciate your
letting others know by leaving a review.

For other wonderful stories,
please visit our on-line bookstore at
www.thewildrosepress.com.

For questions or more information
contact us at
info@thewildrosepress.com.

The Wild Rose Press, Inc.
www.thewildrosepress.com

Stay current with The Wild Rose Press, Inc.

Like us on Facebook

https://www.facebook.com/TheWildRosePress

And Follow us on Twitter
https://twitter.com/WildRosePress